A MAGIC BOAT!

Excitement grew in Lacey as she tried to imagine what the model boat would look like full size. She couldn't help but admire Casey's craftsmanship. "Okay, let's do it," she said, trembling with anticipation.

He nodded. "All right, wish with all your might." He picked up the copper box with two levers on the top. The left one made things big. The right one made things small. He pushed the Get Big lever and stared at the little model on the mound, wishing with all his heart that it would grow.

Casey and Lacey watched breathlessly as they wished and wished. The little boat glimmered and sparkled, followed by a swirling, whirling purple mist. Then came a burst of tiny stars and in the blink of an eye *Hotsy Totsy* became real, as real as the dock the twins stood on.

Lacey's blue eyes widened and she jumped for joy. "Oh, she's beautiful," she gasped in amazement.

OTHER BOOKS YOU MAY ENJOY

CLIVE CUSSLER

The Adventures of
HOTSY TOTSY

PUFFIN BOOKS
An Imprint of Penguin Group (USA) Inc.

PUFFIN BOOKS
Published by the Penguin Group
Penguin Young Readers Group, 345 Hudson Street, New York, New York 10014, U.S.A.
Penguin Group (Canada), 90 Eglinton Avenue East, Suite 700, Toronto, Ontario, Canada M4P 2Y3
(a division of Pearson Penguin Canada Inc.)
Penguin Books Ltd, 80 Strand, London WC2R 0RL, England
Penguin Ireland, 25 St Stephen's Green, Dublin 2, Ireland (a division of Penguin Books Ltd)
Penguin Group (Australia), 250 Camberwell Road, Camberwell, Victoria 3124, Australia
(a division of Pearson Australia Group Pty Ltd)
Penguin Books India Pvt Ltd, 11 Community Centre,
Panchsheel Park, New Delhi - 110 017, India
Penguin Group (NZ), 67 Apollo Drive, Rosedale, Auckland 0632, New Zealand
(a division of Pearson New Zealand Ltd.)
Penguin Books (South Africa) (Pty) Ltd, 24 Sturdee Avenue,
Rosebank, Johannesburg 2196, South Africa

Registered Offices: Penguin Books Ltd, 80 Strand, London WC2R 0RL, England

First published in the United States of America by Philomel Books,
a division of Penguin Young Readers Group, 2010
Published by Puffin Books, a division of Penguin Young Readers Group, 2011

1 3 5 7 9 10 8 6 4 2

THE LIBRARY OF CONGRESS HAS CATALOGED THE PHILOMEL BOOKS EDITION AS FOLLOWS:
Cussler, Clive.
The adventures of Hotsy Totsy / Clive Cussler.
p.   cm.
Summary: Ten-year-old twins Casey and Lacey's adventures continue when
they use their magical machine to turn a model speedboat into a life-size motorboat
to enter a race in San Francisco, and catch the attention of a villain from their past.
ISBN: 978-0-399-25434-5 (hc)
[1. Motorboats—Fiction. 2. Racing—Fiction. 3. Basset hound—Fiction. 4. Dogs—Fiction.
5. Twins—Fiction. 6. Brothers and sisters—Fiction. 7. Magic—Fiction.]
I. Title
PZ7.C965Ach 2010
[Fic]—dc22 2009019130

Puffin Books ISBN 978-0-14-241873-4

Design by Richard Amari
Text set in Wilke Roman

Printed in the United States of America

To my great-grandchildren

when their time comes

to hear and read delightful stories.

Contents

The Adventures of
HOTSY TOTSY

1

The Magic of *Vin Fiz*

The Nicefolk farm, as you may not know or remember, was near the quaint town of Castroville, California, known for its fields of artichokes, a plant whose leaves taste good when heated and dipped in a creamy sauce. But Ever and Ima didn't grow artichokes like all the other farmers in the neighborhood. Their neighbors thought them a little strange because they raised herbs like licorice, spearmint, ginseng and many other exotic varieties that were sold and used in recipes to spice up tasty meals made by gourmet chefs in restaurants from San Francisco to New York to Paris to Hong Kong.

The Nicefolks were good people. Ever was a big man, serious most of the time but with eyes that twinkled. He could always be counted on to help out a neighbor. His wife, Ima, was a sweetheart with a jolly smile that could light up a dark night. For years they had struggled to keep their heads above water by working very hard in the fields. But the past year brought good luck, and now the farm was becoming prosperous.

Casey and Lacey's adventure began when a field-worker showed up one day and asked their father if he could use help for the harvest. He was a tall, lanky man who said his name was Sucoh Sucop, which Lacey quickly discovered was *hocus pocus* spelled backward. He was a gentleman and was accompanied by a donkey named Mr. Periwinkle, who pulled a little red two-wheeled wagon.

Mr. Nicefolk said he couldn't afford hired help, but when the stranger asked for only a place to sleep and his meals, Ever Nicefolk hired him on the spot. From then until the end of the harvest, Sucoh Sucop slept nights in the barn. At least Ever and Ima Nicefolk thought he was sleeping after eating dinner with the family in the house.

The twins knew better.

Something very strange and mysterious was happening inside the barn when the sun fell over the Pacific Ocean to the west. People who passed on the road at night swore they saw strange flickering shadows and an eerie mist surrounding the barn. They also reported an unexplained tingling on their skin.

Casey and Lacey got goose bumps on their arms every time they entered the barn and stood in front of the door to the room Sucoh Sucop lived in. Strangely, the door was always locked. They could not but wonder what secrets were hidden inside.

Finally, when the fields were harvested and the spices packaged and sent on their way, the handyman hitched up Mr. Periwinkle to his little wagon and said his good-byes to the Nicefolk family. Everyone was sad to see him go. Their dog, Floopy, howled as his friend, the little donkey Mr. Periwinkle, and Sucoh Sucop rode off beyond the green fields and disappeared, but not before showing Casey and Lacey what he had been doing nights in the barn. He told them, "You cannot tell nobody what I am about to show you."

Because he swore them to secrecy, they couldn't reveal what they were about to see to anyone, not even their mother and father, because Sucoh Sucop said that grown-up people wouldn't understand. His gift to them, he explained, was to be used only for the children's enjoyment and adventure; anything else and the magic wouldn't work.

With a mystical wizardry the twins never unraveled, Sucoh Sucop had created a machine that could change a tiny object into one that was life-size big. To make the machine work, they had to push a little lever on a black box and wish with all their hearts. On their first attempt they changed a toy tractor into a real tractor. It was big and red and became a true blessing for working the spice farm.

Ever and Ima Nicefolk were astounded and wondered where the tractor came from. Because they were sworn to secrecy by the handyman, the twins simply said it was a present Sucoh left everyone for being so kind to him. Which was really quite true. The few months he was with them, the Nicefolks had taken Sucoh Sucop into their lives as if he was one of the family.

Their next task Casey and Lacey gave to the mysterious machine was to make big a model airplane of the Wright Brothers' *Flyer*, like the one that made the first flight across the United States. They set the model on a large shimmering pad as they had been instructed by Sucop and pushed a lever on an odd-looking box. Then they wished and wished. Before their eyes the model became a real airplane that could actually fly. In fact, because it was so magical it flew itself.

They called it *Vin Fiz* after a grape soft drink Casey liked. Then with Floopy in a box between them, they took off into a blue sky on their great adventure flying across the country.

After they returned, Casey set the mystical pad under the plane and made it into a little model toy again that he hung on a string from the ceiling of his bedroom.

2

The Magic Returns

"School will be out this weekend," said Lacey Nicefolk as she sat on a back porch step and shelled peas from their pods for supper. Lacey was ten years old, with a pretty smile. Her hair was golden amber like her mother, Ima's. She gazed through eyes that were as blue as robin eggs. "We should think about another adventure."

Her brother, Casey, leaned back in a chair and surveyed a model boat he was making.

"I agree with you, sis." Casey was Lacey's non-identical twin since boy and girl twins couldn't be identical. He took after his father, Ever Nicefolk, who had a bushy head of hair as yellow as marigolds and whose sparkly green eyes always seemed to be darting around as if looking for something. "I miss the old *Vin Fiz*. Maybe we should make her large again and take another flight to some exotic lands."

After their great adventure in the *Vin Fiz*, with their long-eared basset hound, Floopy, you would think that freeing the citizens of a town in the desert from desperados, saving the passengers of a Mississippi River steamboat from a great collision, stopping a runaway train and foiling a robbery, not to mention rescuing two girls about to go over Niagara Falls, would be enough adventure to last Casey and Lacey a lifetime. But already life around the farm seemed dull and boring.

"But where?" Lacey loved to ask questions. "Where will we go?" Schoolwork came easy for her. She especially enjoyed solving puzzling problems and analyzing mathematical equations. But she also liked doing things most girls do, dressing up, taking gymnastics and dance classes and helping her mother in the kitchen, especially baking cookies.

Casey was a hands-on kind of boy. He endured school but didn't find it any fun. He preferred working with his hands. Anything mechanical fascinated him. He loved to take things apart and put them back together again, like the farm tractor. He was always tinkering with it. And he loved to build models. The Wright Brothers airplane that he had named the *Vin Fiz* started out as a model before becoming a real life-size flyer.

Casey held up a poster he had sent for through the mail. It showed powerboats racing through the water, making towering rooster tails in their wakes. Big letters across the top of the poster proclaimed:

GOLD CUP GRAND NATIONAL RACE

Forty powerboats expected for the endurance run up the Sacramento River to the state capital and back to the San Francisco Bay marina.

Many great drivers and celebrities will participate in the most spectacular race of the year.

Watch boats speeding over the water in a grueling endurance race of over two hundred miles.

Casey passed the poster to Lacey, who seemed more interested in the colorful boats.

"I thought we might enter this," he said, acting as if he was barely interested. "It looks to be a fine adventure."

"Enter *Vin Fiz* in a powerboat race," Lacey huffed. "That's plain silly."

"Not *Vin Fiz*." Casey held up the model boat. "But a powerboat like this."

"You can't mean that dumb little piece of wood in your hands."

"It's not dumb," Casey said sharply. "This happens to be a model replica of a powerboat that won the Gold Cup races two years in a row," he added proudly.

"It was a long time ago, but I bet it will go as fast as the other boats."

"What do you know about driving in a race with a powerboat?"

"I learned to fly *Vin Fiz*, didn't I?"

"She flew herself," said Lacey, laughing. "You only sat there and held the control stick like a dummy in a store window."

Casey glared at her. "She couldn't have done all those wonderful things without me."

"She flew so high," Lacey said dreamily.

"And she flew so fast," Casey added.

"We could make her big and fly again."

Casey shook his head. "Maybe someday," he said remembering their great flight, "but another adventure could be waiting for us to speed over the water instead of in the air."

Lacey could tell by the look on Casey's face that his mind was set. "When and where is this race?"

"Next Saturday," he replied. "The starting buoy is in San Francisco. The boats travel across the bay and then speed a hundred miles up the Sacramento River to the state capital before coming back again to the starting line at the marina."

"Do you really think your boat can go fast enough to win?" she asked her brother.

"If the mystical machine will give it enough magic, it will," he answered, staring at the model boat in his hands.

Lacey gazed across the fields at the Salinas River, where it ran past the farm on its way to the ocean at Monterey Bay. Thoughtfully, she curled her long golden-amber-colored hair between her fingers. "Mom and Dad are leaving to visit Aunt Polly in San Jose on Thursday. We could start early the next day and use the mystical machine to make the boat big. Then we could cruise up to San Francisco the day before the race, enter the next morning and be home before Mom and Dad the day after."

Suddenly, Floopy began jumping up and down on his short rear legs and barking, his long drooping ears flapping like flags in a Fourth of July breeze.

"See," said Casey, "Floopy wants to go too. I bet he thinks we can win."

Casey and Lacey could see that Floopy knew what they were talking about. He was a basset hound who loved adventure. He had sat in a box between the twins all the way to New York and back on the *Vin Fiz*, and his dog senses told him there was excitement in the air.

Lacey didn't waste time. She was a take-charge girl, and plans for the race were already forming in her mind. She knew what she and Casey had to do.

"You finish your model and make it as perfect as you can," she said, her mind churning. "I'll go to the boat store in town and buy charts showing the coast from here to San Francisco and up the river to Sacramento. They'll be the most important. Speeding up a river will take expert navigation. That will be my job."

Casey wasn't about to let his sister's business-like manner pass by him. "When the time comes, you can also make me a peanut butter sandwich for lunch with a cherry soda. Driving a powerboat makes a man hungry."

Lacey gave her brother a cold look. "You'll be lucky to get bread and water."

Casey ignored her. "We must be careful to make the model into a big boat out of sight of the neighbors. Sucop Sucoh said that if anyone but us knew about the machine, it would never work again."

"We'll be careful," Lacey agreed.

"Then it's a go," said Casey. "Come Friday afternoon, we'll be in San Francisco. On Saturday, we'll be racing up to the state capital with a fleet of powerboats."

But the twins had no idea how complicated entering the race could be. They had no idea there would be entry fees, scads of forms and applications to fill out, an inspection of their boat and documents describing their racing experience. They had the naive notion that all they had to do was show up and speed across the water when the race started.

"It certainly sounds exciting," Lacey said, trying to imagine what it would be like to actually compete against other boats.

The twins shook hands on their coming adventure. Floopy jumped up and down and barked, so they shook his paw too.

That night, after everyone was sleeping, Casey sat in bed under a sheet that was propped up with a stick like an Indian tepee. Using a flashlight, he put the finishing touches on his model powerboat. He secured the steering wheel and fastened the rudder. When he turned the steering wheel lightly, the rudder swung back and forth. Satisfied the sleek little boat was as correct as he could make it, he set it on his nightstand and stared at it, wondering if the mystical machine in the barn could make it speed through the water as *Vin Fiz* had flown through the air.

3

Off to San Francisco

On Friday morning, the day after saying good-bye to her mother and father, Lacey was in the kitchen making peanut butter and jelly sandwiches for the trip. She put the sandwiches and a thermos of cold milk in a backpack along with a few dog goodies for Floopy. After taking five one-dollar bills from a shoe box in her closet, she hurried across the yard to the barn as the first rays of the sun beamed on her golden amber hair. She didn't have to wait more than a minute before Casey walked in carrying the toy boat he had built with loving care. It was a sleek little craft with a tiny cockpit for the crew to sit in and steer. There was even a miniature American flag mounted on a staff in the stern.

"We can't make it big in the barn," said Lacey. "The river is nearly a hundred yards away."

He handed her the boat. "Here, you carry the *Hotsy Totsy*. I'll bring the pad and the mystical box."

She peered at the teeny words Casey had lettered on the bow, which is the front of the boat. "*Hotsy Totsy?* How did you come up with that?"

"It was the name of the powerboat I told you that won the Gold Cup."

"*Vin Fiz,*" Lacey muttered to herself. "And now *Hotsy Totsy.*" She carefully held the fragile little boat in her hands as she walked with Floopy trotting beside her down to the Nicefolk dock, which ran from the shore along the farm thirty feet into the Salinas River. She held the navigation charts of the California coastline and the Sacramento River under her arms.

Casey followed carrying the big shimmering pad over his shoulder and the copper box with two levers in his hands. At the end of the dock, he said, "I'm going to set the boat in a shallow part of the river so she can float."

He took off his shoes and socks and waded into the river until he climbed up a small mound of silt that rose from the bottom. He laid the pad down on the mound and set the copper box on the dock. Then he reached up, took the model boat from Lacey and placed it on the pad. Next, he climbed out of the water and sat on the dock as Floopy, tail wagging, trotted over and licked his face.

Lacey sat down beside Casey and stared at the model powerboat. "How big do you think it will be?" she asked.

"From what I read, *Hotsy Totsy* was a little over twenty-eight feet long by seven feet wide. It had a

V-shaped hull with a shingled bottom like the roof of the farmhouse that made the boat slip easier through the water as it raised the bow."

Excitement grew in Lacey as she tried to imagine what the model boat would look like full size. She couldn't help but admire Casey's craftsmanship. "Okay, let's do it," she said, trembling with anticipation.

He nodded. "All right, wish with all your might." He picked up the copper box with two levers on the top. The left one made things big. The right one made things small. He pushed the Get Big lever and stared at the little model on the mound, wishing with all his heart that it would grow.

Casey and Lacey watched breathlessly as they wished and wished. The little boat glimmered and sparkled, followed by a swirling, whirling purple mist. Then came a burst of tiny stars and in the blink of an eye *Hotsy Totsy* became real, as real as the dock the twins stood on.

Lacey's blue eyes widened and she jumped for joy. "Oh, she's beautiful," she gasped in amazement.

Casey said nothing. He just stared and stared.

Hotsy Totsy was indeed a beautiful boat. Her long lines were sleek and graceful. Her hull, beginning with a small bow, widened as it reached the engine compartment in the middle and began rounding past the cockpit into a torpedo-shaped stern. The wooden hull was formed from dark mahogany and was varnished and highly polished. The seats of her cockpit were covered in a rich red leather. She was built for speed and appeared to be hurtling over the water even though she was sitting still.

Floopy jumped about the dock and barked and barked and barked.

"I'll bet she's fast," said Lacey.

Casey nodded. "The real *Hotsy Totsy* had a big Wright V-12 aircraft engine that could push her over the water faster than any other boats."

Lacey held her hand over her eyes and glanced at the rising sun. She handed Casey a black baseball cap and tied a bandanna around her hair. "We'd better get moving if we want to reach San Francisco and sign up to run in the race."

Casey checked to see if he had his Swiss army knife in his pocket and jumped in the water, waded over to the boat and pushed the bow back and forth until the hull slid off the magic pad. He then hid the magic box and pad under a bush. With the boat moving free in the water, he eased it alongside the dock so Lacey and Floopy could climb down into the cockpit. Then he quickly put on his shoes and socks before studying the instrument panel and the single throttle that was attached to a foot pedal.

"Do you know how to start it?" asked Lacey as she and Floopy settled into the leather seat in the cockpit, anxious to get moving.

CLIVE CUSSLER

"Just like starting the tractor," Casey replied, self-assured.

Lacey had brought life jackets and wouldn't allow Casey to start *Hotsy Totsy*'s engine until they slipped them on. She even settled one around Floopy so they could all float if thrown from the boat. Then she adjusted the seat belts and harness straps that Casey had thoughtfully installed on the model.

Casey pushed the big fuel pedal a half an inch downward. Then he looked for the choke and starter switch. He found them easily because they had little plates under them that labeled what they were. Carefully, cautiously, almost afraid of what would happen, he eased open the choke and pulled the starter switch.

The starter motor began to whine as it turned over the big Wright aircraft engine under the cowl in front of the cockpit. Then came a pop, followed by another

23

pop, and then an entire series of pops inside the twelve cylinders until the engine burst into life with a thunderous roar through the exhaust pipes in the stern.

"She sounds awfully powerful," said Lacey, holding her hands over her ears.

"She's powerful, all right," shouted Casey above the roar. "The original *Hotsy Totsy*'s engine turned out seven hundred and fifty horsepower." He gripped the shift lever that stood upright on the middle of floor and pushed it forward. The gears clunked and the powerboat moved forward, picking up speed as Casey cautiously eased his foot against the pedal.

Although she knew the Salinas River like the back of her hand from many enjoyable trips in their father's little fishing boat, Lacey spread her charts out on her lap and begin studying the riverbanks and the shoals. She wanted to warn Casey if he became excited and steered too close to them.

"Careful not to go too fast down the river," shouted

Lacey. "There are fishermen in their rowboats, so you should stay under ten miles an hour."

"I'll be careful," Casey assured her. "I won't open her up until we come into the bay and enter the ocean."

So far there was nothing magical about *Hotsy Totsy*. She merely responded to Casey's hands on the throttle and steering wheel as he aimed her down the Salinas River into Monterey Bay. She gave no sign of mystical powers or any desire to control her own speed and direction like *Vin Fiz* had on *her* flight across the country.

Lacey could see the eager look on Casey's face. She could tell he was anxious to reach the Pacific Ocean and see how fast *Hotsy Totsy* could go. He kept glancing down at the fuel pedal, which stood nearly two inches above its stop. He held his foot back in anticipation of pushing it all the way to the floor.

At last, after what seemed a week in Casey's mind,

they rounded a bend in the river and cruised into Monterey Bay. The smooth water of the river noticeably changed to choppy as the waves rolled in from the ocean.

"Hold on," he yelled in happy excitement. "Here we go." As he spoke the words, his foot pressed the throttle pedal and slowly pushed it all the way down. As quick as a cat runs through a half-open door, *Hotsy Totsy* lifted her bow and began skimming over the waves, her stern with its spinning bronze propeller whipping through the water. The bow rose until it was two feet above the water as the shingled, V-shaped hull lifted and cut through the waves like a knife, leaving a wide frothing wake that spread behind them.

To protect Floopy's eyes from the spray as the boat bounced over the waves, Lacey slipped a leather helmet with goggles over his head. It was the same helmet and goggles he had worn on the flight of the *Vin Fiz*.

He seemed happy as a lizard on a hot rock with his tongue hanging out one side of his mouth and his ears waggling in the breeze that blew over the small windshield in front of the cockpit.

"How do you like it?" Casey yelled to Lacey.

"Oh, this is great fun," she answered as they passed a sloop under sail as if it was standing still.

They swept past famous Cannery Row in the town of Monterey as Casey steered clear of fishing boats going out to sea to catch mackerel, halibut and cod. Some of the fishing fleet were going after crabs that crawled into wooden traps sitting on the seabed and were attached to a line that stretched upward to a buoy so they could be pulled into the boats.

The fishermen stared in astonishment at the *Hotsy Totsy* as it whisked by them, leaving them rocking to and fro in its wake. They couldn't believe that such a speedy craft was being driven by two children and a funny-looking dog wearing a leather helmet with goggles. Lacey and her brother waved, but the fishermen were too surprised to wave back.

Fortunately for the twins, the summer weather was warm and enjoyable. There was a light mist on the water, common in the morning along the California coast. Casey kept a sharp eye on the rugged coastline so he wouldn't run *Hotsy Totsy* onto the rocks that stretched from the shore. Although he and Lacey were good swimmers, tearing the bottom out of such a beautiful boat and watching her sink below the waves wasn't a calamity he wanted to experience.

"Cut northwest across the bay toward the Santa Cruz lighthouse," directed Lacey. "That should save us a good ten minutes."

"Watch for landmarks," said Casey over the noise of the big Wright engine, "and let me know how we're doing timewise."

Lacey stared through the mist at the cypress and

pine trees filling the cliffs above the sea. Houses that perched in rows above the bluffs came into view, their windows and porches overlooking the ocean. A roadway was dotted with cars whose drivers were taking families out for an early Saturday morning trip. The big lighthouse rose across the bay. "We're coming to Santa Cruz," she called back.

"We're going nearly sixty miles an hour," he said, his eyes darting to a speedometer on the instrument panel.

Lacey estimated their arrival. "With ninety miles to go, we should reach San Francisco Bay in another hour and a half."

Casey merely nodded as the Santa Cruz lighthouse came and went. Lacey looked up at a flight of seagulls that whirled overhead and tried to follow the boat, their wings flapping wildly to keep up. They were joined by ten pelicans who glided above them until they too were outdistanced by the speeding boat.

Dolphins jumped and cavorted as the boat shot past, but they were no match at that speed and quickly fell behind in the churning wake.

"I figure we have less than forty minutes to go," said Lacey, following the coastline on her charts.

Before they knew it, Half Moon Bay was in sight. In less than ten minutes it dropped far behind the stern. Then came the entrance leading to San Francisco Bay. From the surface of the water it looked like a canyon between two high hills. Casey swung *Hotsy Totsy* into the wide channel marked by buoys. The Golden Gate Bridge loomed overhead. As they passed under, they stared up at the immense structure, which was thick with cars traveling from shore to shore. The reddish orange paint shimmered in the light of an early morning sun and reflected off the great towers that supported the cables that held up the highway beneath.

Casey and Lacey had never seen the bridge before

and were thrilled by the sight. They turned their attention to a mammoth aircraft carrier that was approaching with a sea of jet aircraft parked on its sprawling deck. Gazing up as they moved under and along the flight deck, they thought the huge ship looked like a giant gray mountain silently slipping through the water toward the open ocean.

Many of the sailors on board waved at the tiny boat as it sped alongside the carrier's ten-story hull.

Although they had only seen pictures of San Francisco, the twins knew its landmarks by heart. "There's the old prison on Alcatraz Island," shouted Lacey, pointing at the crumbling buildings that once housed evil criminals.

"The Bay Bridge, to Oakland," said Casey, wiping the spray from his eyes to enjoy the view.

"And Treasure Island, where the World's Fair was held."

"Do you see a cable car?"

Lacey shook her head. "Too many buildings in the way."

They gazed at San Francisco's inspiring skyline with its tall buildings and high hills. At last they caught sight of a little cable car slowly moving along shiny rails up a steep incline. Lacey tried to hear the sound of a bell, but the engine under *Hotsy Totsy*'s mahogany cowl made too much noise.

"Let me know when you see the marina," Casey said, his excitement rising. "That's where the starting line is."

"I see an old ferryboat and a sailing ship with tall masts beside a dock off to starboard," she answered, using the nautical word for right. Then she spied a bright mosaic of color that blazed beside a long dock. "There!" Lacey called, pointing at the dock. "A whole fleet of powerboats."

The sleek powerboats were lined up at a long dock.

Several were racing around the bay, tuning their engines for the big race. They were painted in a gleaming luster of colors: bright yellows, greens, blues and reds. Some were even orange and purple. All had the numbers and names of their sponsors lettered on their graceful and streamlined hulls. They all looked as though they could go much faster than *Hotsy Totsy*.

Suddenly a strange-looking powerboat blasted across the water in front of their bow. It was painted jet black but wasn't sleek and graceful like the other boats. There was no lettering on its hull at all. It had the look of an eerie phantom, and it was fast, very fast. It soared over the water like a diving vulture. The vessel bullied its way through the maze of colorful powerboats preparing for the great race and soon disappeared behind Alcatraz Island and the buildings of its famous prison.

"Crazy driver," sputtered Casey as *Hotsy Totsy* was thrown about from the wake of the phantom boat.

"He was certainly in a hurry," said Lacey.

"I wonder if he's in the race."

Lacey looked doubtful. "He had no number, boat name or sponsor logos painted on his hull."

Casey suddenly cocked his head. "Listen to all the noise in the city."

Lacey heard it too. "Sounds like sirens."

"Must be a fire."

Then she pointed over the bow. "There's an open space along the dock," she advised him. "Pull in and we can tie up there."

Casey eased the pedal up to idle speed as he approached the dock and stared at all the boats that were going to race. Hardly an expert powerboat pilot, Casey knocked *Hotsy Totsy* into the tires hanging off the dock as bumpers. Lacey threw lines to a man standing on the dock, who tied the boat to cleats so that it wouldn't float away. He had on the red coveralls worn by the race boat competitors with an insignia patch identifying his boat, called *Bim Bam Boom*. Then the twins lifted Floopy onto the wooden walkway and climbed out of *Hotsy Totsy*.

"If you're coming to watch the race, you'll have to move your boat," said the race boat driver with a smirk. His unruly red hair fell to his shoulders. "This dock is for race contestants only."

"We didn't come here to watch," replied Casey, puffing out his chest. "We came to run *in* the race."

The man began snickering. "Ha, ha," he said in a mocking tone through teeth with a row of gold fillings. "Two little kids in an old boat racing with the pros? That's a laugh."

"Who are you?" asked Casey politely.

"I'm Charley Sploog, and I'm the new champion of powerboat racing. I have the fastest boat. It's called *Bim Bam Boom*."

"What color is it so we know when we pass you?" asked Lacey with a sly grin.

"That will be the day," Sploog said nastily. "Just so you know when you see me win the race, *Bim Bam Boom* is all white."

He turned and walked off laughing, shaking his head in wicked amusement at the twins, their dog and their antique boat.

"He certainly is conceited," Casey muttered.

"A snob, that's for sure," Lacey agreed.

Pretty soon four men, oozing with authority and wearing navy blue blazers, gray slacks and white shirts with bright yellow ties held by little gold powerboat clasps, walked up clutching clipboards with official-looking papers. They each wore a different-colored cap. Casey and Lacey couldn't help but wonder if they were brothers. They all had gray beards with mustaches and large stomachs. All wore oval sunglasses.

The one that Casey assumed was the head race official wore a white cap above saucer-sized ears. He stared at them with a grim wrinkled face and said, "Weren't you kids told to move your boat?"

"Yes, sir," answered Casey, standing taller than he was by lifting his heels off the dock. "But my sister and I are here because we wish to enter the race."

"That's right," said Lacey. "We came all the way from Castroville."

"You can't be serious." The white cap with big ears gasped.

"As serious as can be," said Lacey sweetly.

The second official in a pink cap stared at Floopy through eyes as droopy as the dog's. "You sailed that far along the coast with a hound?"

Casey nodded. "Floopy goes everywhere we go."

"This is one time you aren't going anywhere," said the third race official, whose beady black eyes matched the color of his cap. "Little kids with a droopy-eyed dog in a wooden boat that looks like it belongs in a museum cannot enter a Gold Cup Grand National endurance race and compete with adult professionals in powerboats that can go as fast as one hundred and fifty miles an hour."

The fourth official, who wore a green cap, pulled a ragged cigar from his mouth, smiled with more kindness than the others and said, "You kids better skedaddle home before your parents know what mischief you got into."

"We can win, I know we can win," Casey pleaded.

The official with the white cap grinned wickedly. "Have you got the thousand-dollar entry fee?" He knew very well they probably didn't have a dollar between them.

"You're telling us it costs a thousand dollars just to be in the race?" Lacey said, staring the official in the eyes, her arms clutched in front of her chest, blowing a curl out of her face. She not only looked mad, she was as angry as she had ever been, and she was a girl who was patient and considerate of other people's feelings.

"That's right, little lady," said the green-capped official. "Even if you were old enough and had a super-fast boat, you haven't got the money, and that's that."

"You might as well start for home," said the black-capped official with the beady eyes. "You should have known you couldn't possibly win the one-hundred-thousand-dollar prize that goes to the winner."

Lacey looked at Casey, tears beginning to well in her eyes. "It's not fair."

Casey shrugged and didn't appear dispirited. "No sense in hanging around, sis. We might as well start back to Castroville first thing in the morning."

"See that you're heading for home before the race starts," said Black Cap between chomps on his cigar.

Satisfied they had made their point, the four fat race officials walked away and turned their attention to inspecting a big powerboat that looked like a rocket ship moored behind *Hotsy Totsy*.

"I didn't think you would give up so easily," Lacey said, disappointed with her brother.

Casey gave his sister a fox-like smile. "I have no intention of giving up. We'll make it look like we're leaving for Castroville and then swing back and join the other boats when the starter flare shoots up and race them to Sacramento."

Lacey felt bad for missing her brother's intention. "You had me fooled."

Word soon spread about the boy and girl with their basset hound and antique boat wanting to run in the race. Reporters smelling a human interest story came up and interviewed them. Broadcasters with microphones and cameras asked them all kinds of questions. Satisfied with what they learned, the reporters soon slipped away in search of other stories from the racing teams.

4

The Return of the Boss

"It's them!" hissed an evil-looking man, staring at a TV set that revealed Casey and Lacey being interviewed on the dock.

The man who spoke was tall with an oily mange of black hair and a huge walrus mustache across his upper lip. He wore black from his hat to his shirt to his pants to the boots they were tucked into. Known as the Boss by the police, he was an evil man who robbed and stole from honest people.

Two of the Boss's henchmen, who had crooked teeth and dressed all in black like the Boss, stared at a TV set in the old abandoned warden's mansion at the deserted prison on Alcatraz Island. They were hiding out there after robbing a San Francisco bank and using the race and the powerboats to cover their getaway.

One of them, a man with a wrinkled face who looked like a graveyard salesman, pointed at the screen and said, "The Boss is right. I recognized them right away."

"No, you didn't," said the one with a scraggly beard. "I saw them first."

"You did not."

"Did too."

"Not."

"Too."

"Shut up the both of you," snapped the Boss. "I recognized them before either of you."

The two henchmen looked sullen and glared at each other.

The Boss studied the image of Casey, Lacey and their dog, Floopy, on the TV and twisted the tips of his mustache. "No doubt about it. Those are the brats who caused us to be thrown in jail for holding the townspeople as slaves and making them dig in a mine for a fortune in gold. We'd have gotten away with it if they hadn't flown down in their weird old airplane and spoiled the fun. What did they call that flying antique? Now I remember. It was *Vin Fiz*." His eyes blazed as he watched Floopy walk up and down the pier. "I still carry the marks where that dumb dog with the leather helmet and goggles bit me."

"What should we do, Boss?" asked the bearded henchman.

"We can't do anything for a while. We just robbed five hundred thousand dollars from a bank in San Francisco. We gotta lie low and hide out here in the old abandoned prison buildings until it's safe to escape down the coast to Mexico in our boat."

Wrinkle Face said, "I can't wait to get to Mexico and spend our money."

"Later," the Boss muttered. He twisted his mustache angrily. "I want revenge on those two little brats and their stupid dog. Nobody sends the Boss to jail and gets away with it."

"How can we fix their wagon without the police getting wise?" the Beard asked.

The Boss looked out a dirty window and stared at the water in the bay. "We wait until tonight. Then we sneak over, snatch them and carry them over to our hideout on the island. They'll soon suffer the consequences of what they did to us."

"What does *consequences* mean?" asked a hench-man.

"Something they won't want to think about," answered the Boss with a cold grin.

5

Carried Off into the Night

Lacey spent four of her five dollars from her backpack on two cups of delicious crab with tomato sauce from a huge pot on Fisherman's Wharf. Not having nearly enough money to stay at a hotel, they bedded down under a blanket on the cockpit seat of *Hotsy Totsy*. Lacey used her backpack as a pillow while Casey merely slouched over the steering wheel.

Floopy, finding it too crowded in the boat, curled up in a coil of rope on the dock. Within ten seconds he was fast asleep, growling in dreams only dogs can have.

Almost on the stroke of midnight the phantom

black boat slipped through the inky water alongside *Hotsy Totsy*. She showed no lights and was barely visible under the dim glow from the lamps on the dock. Security guards patrolled along the moored powerboats, whose crews worked through the night to make them ready for the morning's start of the big race. None were near *Hotsy Totsy* when the Boss and his henchmen leaped aboard.

They quickly wrapped Casey and Lacey in blankets and carried them struggling onto the black boat. The children were too shocked to know where they were being taken. Their cries for help were muted by the blankets.

"No sense you brats yelling," the Boss growled. "Nobody is around to hear you."

"Yeah, nobody will hear you," hissed the Beard.

"Can't nobody hear you," echoed the henchman with the wrinkled face.

"I said that," the Beard came back.

"You guys shut up," snapped the Boss at his henchmen, "before the guards get wise."

"Okay, Boss."

"Yeah, Boss."

"Where is the dumb dog?" the Boss snarled. "I
want that dumb dog!"

"He ain't on the boat," Wrinkled Face answered
through yellow teeth.

"Must be up on the dock somewhere," said the
Beard, his whiskers streaked with food stains.

Floopy finally woke up and heard familiar voices.
With a dog's good memory he remembered the harsh
tone of the Boss, who he had bitten only a few months
before. His frantic barks broke the silence.

"Get him!" cried the Boss.

The henchmen climbed onto the dock, but Floopy
was too fast for them. He took off running toward

two security guards who were checking the boats farther down the dock. The evil henchmen couldn't catch him; he was fast for a short-legged, chubby dog.

The Boss shouted, "Get back on the boat before the dog alerts the security guards. We'll come back for him. Let's get out of here."

In less than a minute the sinister boat had vanished into the darkness, taking Casey and Lacey with it.

Floopy ran down the dock to the security guards, yapped and ran back toward the boat.

The guards merely stared at him, more amused than suspicious. Floopy ran back and forth several more times, barking and trying as only a dog can to alert them of the twins' abduction. Nothing worked.

The guards, tired of his antics, began to walk away.

One guard, fat and jolly with his belly hanging over his belt, grinned. "I wonder what's the matter with him."

"Probably those two kids who own him," said the other guard, skinny in a uniform two sizes too big. "They must have taken off for home and forgot him."

"We'll call the dogcatcher in the morning."

"Yeah," replied Skinny. "They'll know what to do with him."

Saddened, his droopy eyes drooping more than ever, Floopy returned to the empty boat at the dock and howled into the night. If dogs could cry, he would have shed a river of tears. He had no idea what to do or where to go. In sorrow, he curled up in the coil of rope in the hope that Casey and Lacey would return.

Floopy lay there, feeling lonely and abandoned. Then his sensitive ears heard something. He lifted his muzzle and cocked his head. A faint rumble seemed to come from the water below the dock. He rose to his four paws and peered over the side. All he saw under the dim light along the dock was the outline of *Hotsy Totsy*. The boat looked dark and empty. Then he spotted blinking lights on the instrument panel and realized the soft rumble came from the big twelve-cylinder Wright engine. *Hotsy Totsy* had magically started the Wright, which was idling softly.

The engine revved several times ever so quietly as if trying to tell Floopy something. He tilted his head as if in thought. He stiffened as he came to realize what *Hotsy Totsy* was trying to tell him.

The speedboat wanted to go after the twins but was secured to the dock.

Floopy ran to the cleat where the bowline was tied. He attacked the cleat with his teeth, pulling it around and around until it came loose and dropped into the water. Then he raced to the bowline and gripped it in his teeth, pulling it from the cleat until it also fell into the water.

Hotsy Totsy revved her engine but didn't shift into gear. She was waiting for Floopy, who was measuring the jump from the dock into the boat. He hesitated a long minute before closing his eyes and leaping through the air. Dropping like the basset hound that he was, his legs came down on the soft leather seats followed by his fat, round body. There was a great thud when he landed, and the boat rocked in the water. Slightly stunned but finding himself all in one piece, Floopy immediately ran to the stern and pulled in the mooring line. Then he rushed to the bow and pulled that line in as well.

No sooner had he jumped down into the cockpit than *Hotsy Totsy* moved away from the dock and over the dark waters of the bay in the direction the phantom boat had vanished.

6

Alcatraz Island

When the black boat came toward the shore of Alcatraz Island, the boss's henchmen opened the doors to the old ferry boathouse. After the boat was moored against the dock inside, the doors were closed and it was as if the phantom craft had never been.

Once they were on the dock, the henchmen removed the blankets from around the children. Casey and Lacey knew it was hopeless to struggle; it had been a tiring day and they had to fight to keep from falling asleep. They stumbled as they were pushed by the Boss and his henchmen out of the ferry boathouse and under the catwalks and guard towers.

Lacey turned and saw a full moon setting beyond the Golden Gate Bridge across the bay. A light breeze moved the waves, and she could hear the bell on a buoy somewhere on the black water. She wondered what would become of Floopy and *Hotsy Totsy* if she and Casey never returned.

"Where are you taking us?" demanded Casey, coming back on track.

"To the main cell house. I've got a nice little cell all picked out for you," snarled the Boss. "Plenty of rust and grime. Plenty of old rot. Plenty of rats. A famous gangster by the name of Al Capone used to live in it."

"Who was Al Capone?" asked Casey.

"A very bad man who was the crime lord of Chicago many years ago." The Boss paused to snicker evilly. "You'll soon be wishing you was back in your beds at home. Oh, and I almost forgot. There are no meals here."

"You want us to starve?" asked Lacey, growing angry.

"Yes, and I'll enjoy every minute of it."

"But why?"

"For getting me and my gang thrown in jail when you flew that old ratty airplane into Gold City, Nevada. I had a good thing going there, forcing the townspeople to mine gold, but you brats had to interfere and call in the cavalry, who arrested us and threw us in a jail in the middle of the desert. And then there was my brother, the Chief, and his gang of bandits, who you brats and that stupid dog also got thrown in jail. You're all going to pay for that."

Casey stood tall and looked the Boss in the eye. "What if we escape?"

The Boss smiled like a fox. "No one ever escaped from Alcatraz and lived to tell about it."

"How did you escape from jail?"

"My henchmen and I carved fake guns out of wood

and coated them with black shoe polish. We fooled the guards, who surrendered, locked them in our cells and made off in the warden's fast car."

"Why are you here?" asked Casey. "The police will look for you on the island."

"Alcatraz is deserted. The government closed it down for restoration, which hasn't begun yet. There's no one on the island but us."

"At least Floopy got away," Lacey said testily.

The Boss rubbed his hands and grinned fiendishly. "I'll catch him tomorrow."

"You'll never find Floopy, much less catch him," Lacey said defiantly.

"I'll get him," snarled the Boss. "Just you wait and see."

"What will you do with him?" Casey demanded.

The Boss laughed wickedly. "Just you wait and see."

7

Locked in a Dungeon

The Boss had kept his word. Casey and Lacey were locked in a smelly and dirty cell. There was a moldy bunk with a mattress, but they kicked it on the floor rather than lie on it and sat on the rusty springs. This was an event the twins never thought would happen in their wildest imaginations. They had assumed the Boss and his henchmen were still in jail, along with his brother, the Chief, and his bandits.

"This place is awful," said Lacey as she pulled her sweater over her shoulders and shivered. "It's cold and it's damp in here. It was a big mistake to leave home and try to enter some dumb old race."

"It seemed like a good idea at the time," Casey argued. "We might have won."

"Is that all you can think about?"

"There are other things," Casey fumed.

"I'm not as worried about us as I am about what will happen if that terrible Boss gets his hands on Floopy," said Lacey mournfully.

"He won't if *Hotsy Totsy* carries him away."

"But our speedboat is tied to the dock. She can't move."

"Then we've got to get out of here," Casey said in a determined voice.

Lacey looked doubtful. "You heard what the Boss said. No one ever escaped from Alcatraz and lived to tell about it."

Casey didn't answer as he studied the bars facing the interior of the cell block.

Lacey leaned an arm and shoulder between the bars. "We're a lot smaller than Al Capone must have been. If we could bend or remove one bar, we could squeeze through."

Casey kicked at the bar. It was old and not as stout as it once was. Rust flakes flew off and settled on the cell floor. "It looks weakened with age. If we had a saw, we could cut through it."

"But we don't have a saw," Lacey reminded him.

"Yes," said Casey sadly. "I guess we'll never get out of here. What will our poor mother and father do when we never come home?"

"I'll bet I can make a saw."

Casey looked at his sister. "You can what?"

"Make a saw. Do you still have your Swiss army knife?"

He reached in his pocket, pulled out the knife and held it up.

"Now take it and scrape the blade against a concrete block in the wall. Use that old newspaper on the floor to collect the concrete dust."

Casey didn't question his sister and did as he was told. He knew she was smart, smarter than him, especially in school. He began scraping the concrete dust into the newspaper.

Lacey looked into her backpack and pulled out a tube of glue she always carried and some string. She wiped the glue onto the string and then rolled the string in the concrete dust falling on the newspaper until it was covered from tip to tip.

"Very clever of you, sis. I see now that you want to make a string saw."

She nodded. "As soon as the glue dries, we wrap the string around the bar and begin sawing away while the concrete dust acts as an abrasive."

"We'll need more than one before we're finished," said Casey. "While I cut the bar, you make more string saws."

Unknown to Casey and Lacey, *Hotsy Totsy,* with Floopy sitting on the bow, had cruised across the bay and stopped at the ferry house. Floopy managed to grip the latch in his teeth and very quietly opened the doors. Next he jumped out onto the dock with a line in his mouth and wrapped it around a cleat. Then, using his very sensitive dog nose, he sniffed the familiar smells of Casey and Lacey and began running up the road toward the big cell house, following their scent.

Floopy ran up the concrete stairs onto the parade field, then around the road past the warden's mansion, where the Boss and his henchmen were hiding out. Through an open window, he saw men moving. He stopped for a moment, sniffing. Detecting the familiar scent of the Boss, Floopy remembered sinking his teeth into the evil villain's behind and wagged his tail. Padding softly, with only his nails clicking on the ground, he turned and nosed up the walkway that led to the porch of the mansion. When he reached the front door, he crept around up to the open window and stared inside.

The Boss and his henchmen were sitting around eating a leftover Chinese takeout dinner and watching a cartoon on television. After a few minutes, the Boss turned off the picture and held up a map.

"Here's how we make our getaway," he explained. "We wait until dark tomorrow night. Then we take our boat and move without lights under the Golden Gate Bridge. Once outside the bay, we head south to Mexico. After we cross the border, the police will never catch us."

"What about the kids?" asked the Beard.

"Who cares," the Boss barked. "By the time they're found, we'll be long gone."

"What about the dog?" asked Wrinkle Face.

"He'll be lost without those brats and will probably end up begging on the streets."

Floopy couldn't understand English or read, but he knew the Boss was saying something unpleasant about Casey and Lacey and he growled.

The Boss tensed. "Did you hear something?" he asked his henchmen.

"Sounded like the wind," said the Beard.

"No," came back Wrinkle Face. "It was a boat horn."

"Wind."

"Horn."

"Shut up, both of you," snapped the Boss. "It was a dog. I'd know that growl anywhere. It was that dog with the helmet and goggles that bit me in Nevada. He's here on the island. You two, quick, go out and catch him."

The henchmen looked at the Boss and then at each other, not sure they had heard him right.

"Don't stand there like a pair of goony birds! Get going!"

The Beard and Wrinkle Face took off out the door and across the porch where Floopy was lying. They both tripped over him and spilled down the stairs in a heap of arms and legs, grunting like mad bears. The

Boss dashed through the door to see what happened. Just as he reached the top of the stairs, Floopy leaped up and bit him on the seat of his pants. The Boss yelled in pain.

"Oh no, not again!"

But before he could kick Floopy, the dog had sprung from the porch and scurried into the night.

The Boss held his hands to his torn pants and glared down at his henchmen. "Go after him! He can't get far!"

"Maybe he's going for the kids," said the Beard.

"Won't do him any good," said the Boss. "No way a dog can open doors and get into the cell house, much less open the brats' locked cell door."

"What'll we do, Boss?" asked Wrinkle Face.

"Get flashlights, then split up and search the grounds. There's no place he can hide."

8

Escape from Alcatraz

Following the twins' scent, Floopy ran up to the entrance of the cell house. It was a big steel door that looked impossible for a dog to open. He stood on his hind legs and pushed with his front paws. There came a soft creak from the hinges. He moved back and looked up with his head tilted in puzzlement. He wondered why the big steel door creaked. Standing there, he tried to think like a human. Then it came to him. If the door creaked, it must be unlocked.

Floopy stood again and pushed with all his might. This time the creak came louder and the door moved an inch. Not knowing about such things, Floopy didn't realize that the bolt hadn't gone into the catch when the Boss's henchmen thought they locked the door. Again he pushed against the door, using all the strength he had. Slowly the big steel door's creak turned into a big squeak and it moved open another six inches, making an opening of seven inches. Although Floopy was hefty for a dog so close to the ground, seven inches was all he needed to squeeze between the opening and wiggle into the cell house.

Casey and Lacey set to work, taking turns at furiously pulling the ends of their string saws back and forth around one of the bars. The plan was working. The concrete powder glued to the strings cut into the old, rusty bar. But it was slow work, very slow work, and they went through each string saw after only a few minutes.

"How are we doing?" asked Lacey, making another string saw while Casey pulled the ends of the string one way and then the other.

"We're cutting a groove, but we have a ways to go," he answered between breaths.

Just then they heard barking down below on the bottom floor of the cell house.

"Floopy!" Lacey burst out. "That can only be Floopy!"

It was true—Floopy had a very distinctive woof, low and almost musical.

"Here, Floopy!" Casey shouted. "Up here!"

"Hurry, Floopy!" cried Lacey.

Floopy's tail began wagging wildly at the sound of his beloved friends' voices. He sniffed their trail up the stairs and down the catwalk to their cell. He arrived, his tongue hanging out and panting from his run through the prison yard.

"Oh, Floopy," cried Lacey. "How did you ever get here across the bay?"

Not being able to answer, Floopy frantically licked the twins' faces, he was so glad to see them.

"He must have been carried over the water by *Hotsy Totsy*," reasoned Casey. "She must be waiting at the ferry building."

Lacey reached through the bars and hugged her dog. Then she noticed something in Floopy's mouth. She pulled it away and saw that it was a piece of cloth. "What's this?" she asked, looking into Floopy's big brown eyes.

"Looks like a piece of the Boss's pants," Casey said with a big smile growing across his lips.

Lacey threw the piece of torn pants on the bed as she scratched Floopy's long ears. "That means the Boss knows Floopy is on the island looking for us. He must be crazy mad after being bitten."

"Not the first time either," recalled Casey.

"The Boss will come to check on us as sure as there is a sun and moon," Lacey said, becoming fearful. "No telling what he'll do if he catches Floopy with us."

"We've got to get out of here quick." Casey took up a string file and began desperately rubbing it against the bar. "You cut on the top of the bar while I cut on the bottom."

For the next five minutes Casey and Lacey pulled the string files, filled with a sense of urgency. By now their hands were tired and sore.

"We'll never make it," Lacey said wearily.

Casey didn't look defeated. "We'll need another twenty minutes before we cut all the way through the bar," he said. "With Floopy's help we can try and force the bar to break off."

"How can Floopy help?" wondered Lacey.

"You keep cutting while I take a spring off the bed,

stretch it out and wrap one end around the bar and the other around Floopy's collar."

Lacey saw the genius in her brother's thinking and clapped. "You're a wizard," she said.

He laughed. "I only wish I was a wizard."

Casey soon twisted a spring off the lower bed, wrapped it around the bar and attached the other end to Floopy's collar. "Okay," he said to his sister. "Lie down and we'll both kick the bar as hard as we can while Floopy pulls from his side."

Floopy knew what was expected of him and leaned forward, pulling with all his might.

On the other side of the bars, the twins kicked as hard as they could.

At first nothing happened. The bar seemed as solid as ever and didn't bend.

"Harder!" Casey called out. "We've got to try harder."

This time they gave it all they had while Floopy

dug his paws into the concrete floor and pulled and pulled. Just as it seemed they were wasting their time, suddenly the top piece of the bar broke loose. Now they gained extra pressure by bending the top half of the bar outward. It snapped and fell to the floor with a loud twang. Casey helped Lacey through the opening in the bars and quickly followed.

"We're free!" Lacey said with great relief.

"We'll have to hurry if we want to reach the ferry house before the Boss and his henchmen find us," Casey urged his sister. "*Hotsy Totsy* will carry us back across the bay."

They ran down the catwalk, ran down the stairs, ran through the cell block and out the big steel door. Although there were no lights except from the moon and the streets of San Francisco, they followed the white tip of Floopy's tail, knowing he would lead them straight to *Hotsy Totsy*. They darted across the parade grounds and dashed down the steps into the ferry house. It was almost completely black inside, but they could make out their beloved speedboat tied to the dock where Floopy had left her.

The Boss and his henchmen couldn't find Floopy. Finally, the Boss sat down, catching his breath from running all over the prison grounds.

"We've looked everywhere," he said. "Where could that stupid dog be?"

"He must have been looking for them kids," said the Beard.

"Nay," mumbled Wrinkle Face. "You locked the main door to the cell house."

"I didn't lock it. You did."

"Did not. You did."

"Not."

"Did."

"Are you idiots telling me you forgot to lock the main door?" yelled the Boss.

The Beard shrugged. "No big deal. Those kids can never escape from Al Capone's old cell."

"That's true," the Boss agreed. "But we'd better check on them just to be sure."

It didn't take long for them to find an empty cell and a rusted steel bar lying on the floor.

"They've—they've become invisible," stammered Wrinkle Face.

"Fools, they sawed through the bar and escaped. That stupid dog must have helped them."

The Beard shook his head dumbly. "Where could they go?"

Wrinkle Face shook his head dumbly too. "They can't swim across the bay at night."

"The dog must have somehow come over on their boat," said the Boss. "Quick! We've got to hightail it to the ferry house before they can escape."

*   *   *

Lacey and Floopy untied the lines and jumped from the dock into the cockpit of *Hotsy Totsy*, but Casey didn't follow them. He stood quietly studying the phantom black boat that was tied up on the opposite side of the dock.

"Aren't you coming?" Lacey demanded, expecting the Boss and his henchmen to come running into the ferry boathouse at any moment.

Casey made no reply. He jumped down into the black phantom boat, opened the cowling and disappeared into the engine compartment. Lacey could hear sounds of metal clinking on metal and then all was silent. Then came a loud clunk followed by Casey, who closed the cowling and leaped into *Hotsy Totsy*.

As he settled behind the wheel, the magical boat started its own engine and began moving slowly out of the ferry boathouse. They had only gone about ten feet from the dock when the Boss and his henchmen came running through the door.

"They're getting away!" shouted the Boss, stopping at the edge of the dock and shaking his fist. "Get our boat started. We've got to stop them before they give us away to the police."

Casey didn't waste a second. As soon as they were clear of the building and out in the bay, he pushed the fuel pedal to the floor and sent *Hotsy Totsy* speeding over the inky water toward the lights of San Francisco.

Seconds later, the Boss, the Beard and Wrinkle Face jumped into the black phantom speedboat. Imagine their surprise when they found themselves splashing into water that was rising above the front seat.

"Our boat is sinking," said the Beard, stunned.

"Check the engine!" commanded the Boss, his anger mounting.

The henchmen threw back the engine cowling and shined flashlights inside.

"The water is already two feet deep in the engine compartment," came back Wrinkle Face. "No way we can start it."

"Those rotten brats opened the drain plugs!" the Boss bawled out. "Shut them off and turn on the bilge pumps. They'll be sorry for this. I'll make their lives miserable for messing with the Boss."

Out in the bay, Lacey kept turning around, looking for the Boss's black phantom boat. They would have to run with lights, she reasoned, if they were to find and catch *Hotsy Totsy*. Amazed that she saw no sign of the evil men and their boat, she looked at Casey.

"They don't seem to be following us," she said thankfully. "Do you know why?"

Casey smiled from ear to ear. "They never left the ferry house. I opened their drain plugs. It will take them a good ten minutes to pump enough water out of the boat to start the engine."

"So that's why you jumped into the black boat," said Lacey, proud of her brother.

"Soon as we dock, we'll call the police and tell them where to find the thieves and the stolen bank money. I wish I could see their faces when they're caught," said Casey.

Lacey grinned. "I'm only glad we weren't there when they found their boat sinking at the dock," she said.

"I'll bet the Boss was so mad he could spit." Casey laughed.

"Yuck, I wouldn't want to see that."

While the Beard and Wrinkle Face worked at pumping water out of the boat, the Boss ran back to the warden's mansion and retrieved the stolen bank money. He returned to the ferry boathouse as his henchmen finished fixing the drain plugs and pumped the water from the hull.

They looked pleased with themselves. "All ready to start her up and head after those kids," said the Beard.

"Forget those brats." The Boss snorted. "They must be across the bay by now and calling the cops."

Wrinkle Face asked, "Are we heading out to sea and down to Mexico?"

The Boss shook his head. "A change of plans. The cops will have every Coast Guard boat and helicopter searching the coast for us. Instead, we're going to join the powerboat race tomorrow."

The Beard and Wrinkle Face stared at each other, confused. "Won't that be like putting up a flag and saying come get us?" muttered the Beard.

The Boss grinned wickedly. "Not if we go up the Sacramento River tonight and hide out in the trees along the bank. Then, after the boats refuel at the city docks and continue on the return run down the river, we join the boats as they race past. Our boat is as fast as any of them, so we'll have little trouble catching the brats and smashing them, that dumb dog and their boat into teeny-tiny pieces."

"But they won't be in the race with their old wooden boat," said Wrinkle Face. "The officials will never let them enter."

"I know those brats," said the Boss. "They never do what they're told. Those twins and their stupid dog will be in the running, just you wait and see."

"Gee, the Boss is one smart boss," said Wrinkle Face.

"Good thinking, Boss," came back the Beard.

The Boss threw the suitcase with the stolen money into the cockpit. "Start the engine. I want to find a good place to hide along the river before the sun comes up."

After they docked, the twins told their story to the security guards, and the police were called to take them to the nearest station to fill out a report on their scrape with the Boss. Casey and Lacey were thrilled to ride through the city streets in a patrol car, its siren shrieking.

The chief detective, whose name was Mulroony, reminded Lacey of the giant who lived on the beanstalk. He was a tough-looking man, but a kindly one. He smiled and offered the twins candy as he read their report. Finally, he glanced up with a solemn look on his face.

"We sent a squad over to Alcatraz, but there was no sign of the Boss or his henchmen. They and their boat were gone. They're probably in the ocean, speeding toward Mexico."

"Did they really rob a bank?" asked Casey.

Mulroony nodded. "They got five hundred thousand dollars from the Nob Hill Bank."

"I'm sorry I couldn't have caused more damage to their boat," Casey said sadly.

"Don't feel bad," Mulroony said slowly. "You did

your best." He stood up, leaned over and petted Floopy. "Now you kids run along and get some sleep. If we need any more information, we can call on you in Castroville."

The patrol car took the twins back to the dock. They went aboard *Hotsy Totsy* and were soon fast asleep.

9

Thunder Across the Bay

They had slept only a few hours when they were awoken by the loudspeaker announcement instructing the drivers to start their engines. Casey yawned and lifted Floopy out of the coil of rope that had become his bed and handed him down to Lacey. Then he got busy untying the lines to the dock. Once behind the wheel, he started the engine and moved toward the Golden Gate Bridge and the sea.

Hotsy Totsy moved through the water slowly toward the sea as if they were leaving San Francisco. A fancy yacht with the officials passed them and took up station at the starting line. Lacey counted forty-two boats that moved around in circles as they lined up for the start of the race. At a signal from the officials on the yacht, the pilots would launch a vast free-for-all across the bay toward the entrance of the Sacramento River.

A sea of pleasure boats had already lined up along both sides of the course, which was marked by yellow buoys. A thousand spectators were in a festive mood, many dining on goodies from picnic baskets as they waited for the flare to shoot into the sky from the official yacht that would signal the start of the Gold Cup Grand National Race.

The brilliant colors of the powerboats caught the morning sun and sparkled like Christmas ornaments on the blue-green water. The thrill of excitement was in the air as the pilots revved their powerful engines, the exhaust sounds going from a muffled throb to a low gurgling growl. Now all the boats broke out of the circle and headed slowly toward the start line so they could sneak into a good position to get the jump on the other boats and make a clean getaway.

The orange flare signaling the one-minute warning shot into the blue sky as the pilots looked left to right and back again, seeing how far they were spaced apart. The pack was building into a stampede across the bay. Their big one-thousand-horsepower engines roared as the drivers surged toward the starting line in the same instant the chief official in the white cap raised his hand that held the flare gun.

Unnoticed, *Hotsy Totsy* moved slowly behind the official yacht and approached from its stern. The race officials were looking the other way as they watched the boats gather in a rough lineup for the start. The excitement was building, but the boat pilots and the thousands of spectators failed to notice *Hotsy Totsy* suddenly rushing forward behind the fleet. Then the green flare was shot into the air and exploded with green streamers against a white-clouded sky.

The race was on.

Like a Thoroughbred leaping from the starting gate, *Hotsy Totsy* dug her stern in the water, lifted her bow and leaped over the water into the wake of the powerboats that were cutting across the bay like multicolored missiles.

As they hurtled past the official yacht, Lacey grasped one of Floopy's paws and waved it at the race officials, who were frantically trying to wave them off the course. At first it seemed as though they needn't have bothered. *Hotsy Totsy* was quickly being left behind in the wakes of the much-faster boats.

"She'll never keep up," cried Lacey miserably. "She isn't nearly fast enough. Maybe we were wrong to bring her here."

"She can do it," Casey said gamely. "I know she can. If *Vin Fiz* did it, so can *Hotsy Totsy*."

Lacey peered through the windshield and saw that

the field of boats was halfway across the bay. "Speed!" Lacey pleaded. "Speed like the wind . . . please."

Magically, as if *Hotsy Totsy* knew what she must do, her big Wright engine whirled into a screeching whine and spun the bronze propeller into a blur that cut through the water at a speed that pressed the twins and Floopy against the seats. She took off like a shell out of a cannon. In almost no time she was passing the boats trailing the main pack.

"*Hotsy Totsy* has the same magic as *Vin Fiz*," shouted Casey, overjoyed.

Lacey held her arms tightly around Floopy's neck as he barked from joy. "It's so wonderful," she shouted back.

Hotsy Totsy had become a part of them. Casey and Lacey no longer had any doubts that she had a mind of her own and was going to use all her magical powers to win the race.

The pleasure boats and expensive yachts formed a corridor for the boats roaring across San Francisco Bay. Casey and Lacey were stunned by the number of people watching from their boats. Everyone was waving and cheering them on.

The gleaming white *Bim Bam Boom* burst into the lead as the herd swept under the Oakland Bay Bridge and past Treasure Island. *Hotsy Totsy* pulled between two boats. One was rose-colored, the *Tickled Pink*, and the other, the *Twitter Tweet*, was painted a flashy lavender. The green water of the bay had turned white with froth as the spinning propellers of the boats shot it into the air in vast swirling waves. To see so many powerful boats speeding at over a hundred miles an hour was an incredible sight no one who saw it would ever forget.

The first-turn marker buoy, a yellow one in the shape of a tall glass of lemonade, was coming up, and the pilots prepared to cut a turn without slowing down. Trailing, but beginning to move up, *Hotsy Totsy* kissed the waves from the wakes of the front-running boats as lightly as if she was sailing through a field of feathers.

Casey didn't have to work the throttle. *Hotsy Totsy* controlled her speed up and down depending on the traffic while all Casey had to do was steer between the other boats.

"She's running smooth!" yelled Casey. He saw the other boats dive into the three-foot-high waves from the wakes of the leaders. Not *Hotsy Totsy*. Her bow lifted over them and her V-shaped hull cut right through. But Casey almost spoke too soon. Two other boats sliced in front of him to sweep around the first marker buoy of the course.

"They're cutting us off!" screamed Lacey as the apricot orange *Rat Tat Tat* zigzagged in front of *Hotsy Totsy*, showering the twins and Floopy in a watery surge that flooded the cockpit and soaked everyone in it. Floopy snarled at the other boats, showing his teeth, and then looked down in the water slopping around the cockpit floor as if he was searching for a fish.

Casey was wiping his face, the salt water stinging his eyes. "I can't see, I can't see!" He was also blinded by the huge spray sent up from the propeller of *Tickled Pink*, which swung directly in front of *Hotsy Totsy*'s bow. "Steer until I can see again," he ordered Lacey.

But before Lacey could grab the wheel, the powerboat was thrown violently from side to side and it was all Lacey could do to put an arm around Floopy and hold on to the cockpit seat to keep both of them from being flung into the bay. Thank heavens for the belts and harnesses, she thought.

The driver of *Rat Tat Tat* threw an insulting wave and could be seen laughing at the water-soaked twins.

"They're doing it on purpose!" snapped Casey, his

left eye beginning to focus. He shook a fist at the boats speeding in front of *Hotsy Totsy* that had sprayed them with sheets of water. "You'll be sorry," he muttered to himself. "*Hotsy Totsy* will make you sorry for being nasty."

To the spectators, the two modern powerboats speeding around the magical powerboat hull to hull and closing in front of them at over one hundred miles an hour was a breathtaking sight. One that Casey and Laccy would always remember. Suddenly, their boat struck the combined wakes of the two boats ahead and *Hotsy Totsy* was spun out of control. Casey finally managed to see out of both eyes again but couldn't see through the sheet of spray that blew into them. He thought he heard Lacey screaming through the deafening sounds around him, but he wasn't sure.

Knowing he couldn't hear her warning, she leaned over Floopy and yelled in Casey's ear, "Left! Turn left!"

In that instant he could see they were hurtling through the water toward one of the spectator boats, a huge luxurious yacht that looked as big as an ocean liner. He spun the wheel to the left as Lacey had warned and tried but failed to pull back the throttle. The crew and guests on board the yacht looked at the boat rushing toward them with horror. There seemed no way to avoid a terrible disaster. The twins could do nothing but sit in shock before they crashed.

But then a miracle happened.

Hotsy Totsy drove across the wake of the power-boats, riding up the waves, and leaped out of the water skyward. The little craft soared into the air. It soared over the yacht, and the people stared in amazement as it flew over their heads. They scattered over the decks and tried to hide. The twins couldn't believe a boat could fly so high into the air and so far before it crashed down in the water, burying the bow and boring through a wall of solid liquid until the bow burst free and shot upward.

"*Hotsy Totsy* truly is a magical boat," yelled Lacey excitedly as the powerboat spun around the pleasure yachts, moved past the marker buoy and took up the chase again.

"She's as magical as *Vin Fiz*," Casey agreed.

"And then some!"

Hotsy Totsy didn't need to be told to hurry. Like a fast racehorse that got off to a bad start, she dug in her propeller, lifted her bow and took off after the power-boats like a torpedo through turbulent water. She passed *Swizzle Swish*, whose pilot and copilot stared disbeliev-ing as the old speedboat tore past. Next came *Tickled Pink*, whose pilot laughed as *Hotsy Totsy* came along-side. Casey timed it so that as soon as his stern was ten feet ahead of the other boat, he cut across its bow and let his wake drench the other crew.

"That was awfully close," said Lacey.

"A taste of their own medicine," answered Casey. "Where are we now?"

Lacey consulted her charts and compared their course with the landmarks on the shore. "We just passed the prison at San Quentin. The bridge up ahead is the Richmond–San Rafael Bridge. Once we go under, we head into San Pablo Bay."

A few boats were already dropping out of the race and leaving the course. Smoke was trailing from under the engine cowling on the green-and-red-striped *Suzie Wuzie* as she limped off the course. They roared past an upside-down *Squeaky Klean*. The crew were in the water as the rescue boat hurried toward them. They waved their arms and hands to signal that they were all right. Another boat with gold lightning bolts painted across the hull was stopped off to the side of the course with a dead engine.

"How are we doing?" Casey asked Lacey, unable to take his eyes off the boats ahead and around him.

Lacey did a rough count of the boats she could see through the clouds of spray. She deducted the ones she saw that had left the race and surveyed those in the front and to their rear.

"As near as I can make it, we're running in thirty-fourth place."

"Then we've passed eight boats," Casey said cheerfully. "*Hotsy Totsy* can do it. I know she can be the first over the finish line."

"Look!" called out Lacey. "There's an official boat ahead. Someone is waving a flag. I think they're waving at us."

"What color is it?"

"Black, it's a black flag."

"I wonder what it means."

"I think they want us to drop out of the race," Lacey said angrily.

"No way," Casey said, steadfast.

They tore by a white boat marked with a variety of

flags. An official standing on the stern violently waved a black flag in their direction. Lacey simply waved back at him, secretly enjoying watching him jump up and down on the deck looking so aroused in a vain attempt to stop the twins from racing.

Hotsy Totsy gained a rhythm over the wakes of the front-running boats and gained on the leaders with every mile. She and Casey soon learned to run and drive smoothly despite the boats and their pilots blocking their passage and playing collision tactics, only pulling away at the last instant before crashing into *Hotsy Totsy* and crushing her wooden hull.

Casey was a fast learner and soon learned to give as good as he received. He refused to back down and dared other boats to force him off the course or drown him in their wakes. Together, he and the boat quickly figured out the race tactics that were thrown at them. They went from amateurs to professionals within twenty miles.

Hotsy Totsy and the twins were almost across San Pablo Bay when Lacey pointed over the windshield at a red buoy coming up on their port (nautical for "left") side. "There's the buoy marking the turn for the entrance to the Sacramento River," she yelled to Casey.

Abruptly, a boat in front of them began to slow down. It was a sleek red, white and blue powerboat named *Uncle Sam*. Its throttle cable had split apart, and the engine slowed as it fell into an idle. Casey made it past *Uncle Sam* but came so close he drenched the crew with a huge wake from *Hotsy Totsy*'s stern. He lifted both hands in a helpless gesture that meant he was sorry.

The other crew understood and courteously waved as Casey shot ahead.

Casey became a little nervous since he was being pushed into a very tight turn around the buoy by three other boats battling to get around first. The orange *Rat Tat Tat*, white *Whizzard* and apple green *Vroom*

Vroom along with *Hotsy Totsy* were four abreast as they entered the turn around the buoy. Casey was tempted to stay alongside the other boats and not be bullied, but they were coming closer and closer, squeezing the little mahogany boat between them. *Hotsy Totsy* sensed exactly what to do. Without Casey pulling back on the throttle, she slowed and let the other boats slip in front of her. Then her big Wright engine bellowed out with full power.

Hotsy Totsy darted to the outside of the pack and made a sharp turn fast and tight, coming out ahead once she rounded the buoy. It was a daring and brilliant tactic and it worked. The twins and their boat had moved up three more places. Not only had the magical little powerboat come out in front of the group, she was pulling away. The gap between them was widening, and now Casey set his sights on the crowd of powerboats still in front of their bow.

Word of the boy and girl and their basset hound

running in the race with an old wooden boat swept up and down the thousands of spectators in pleasure yachts and those lining the shore. Nothing fires excitement more in a sporting event than the hope that an underdog just might win.

As they swept out of San Pablo Bay and under the bridge between Crockett and Vallejo, the twins could see crowds of onlookers waving wildly and cheering them on.

"Look, Casey," cried Lacey. "Everyone is rooting for us."

Floopy sensed the inspiration coming from the shore by the barking and yapping of the spectators' dogs. He barked back and jumped up and down with his long ears waving back at the dogs and their owners. Lacey had to clutch Floopy or he would have jumped out of the boat. He reacted wildly when a helicopter swooped low over *Hotsy Totsy* with TV cameras focused on the occupants of the powerboat.

It was almost as if he knew he was on camera and began acting like a human, sitting up on the seat and waving his paws.

"I hope we're not recognized," said Lacey. "Mom and Dad won't be happy if they find out what we've done."

"Don't worry," Casey replied, pulling his baseball cap low on his forehead as his fingers tightened on the steering wheel despite the fact that *Hotsy Totsy* seemed in complete control. "They'll never know where we could get a boat this fast. If they happen to watch the race on TV, they'll think it's some other kids with a funny dog. Just don't look up at the cameras and wave."

From then on whenever a news helicopter flew over or they passed boats hired by TV stations, they ducked down in the cockpit so their faces couldn't be seen on camera, not realizing that by hiding their faces, they created more interest. A mystery began building around the entire country as millions of people watching the race on television sets at home couldn't help but be fascinated by the odd-looking boat and its mysterious little occupants.

"Here comes another official race boat," Lacey alerted Casey.

"Ignore them. They can't stop us now."

This time, as they passed an obviously stressed race official fiercely waving a black flag at them, Lacey stuck out her tongue at him. Angered that his attempt to stop the powerboat was ignored, he got even angrier at seeing Lacey make faces at him and threw the flag down on the deck of the boat and stomped on it. As *Hotsy Totsy* whipped past the official boat, Casey and Lacey, normally courteous and thoughtful, couldn't help laughing.

"He didn't look happy," said Casey.

"They just don't understand that we're not going to quit," Lacey said seriously.

"We're in the race from start to finish. Nicefolks never quit."

On board the official boat the race director, who had tried to black-flag the twins, was madder than a crab in a trap. "How are we going to stop those crazy kids?" he asked another race official.

A man wearing a captain's cap with a braid and a blue blazer pointed up at the news helicopter. "Because of those kids and their old boat, we're generating more interest in the race than if the president of the United States was here."

The race director stared at *Hotsy Totsy* as it roared up the river. He looked at the television cameras mounted atop trucks along the riverbanks. "Yes," he agreed reluctantly. "More people are watching this race than ever before. But regardless of the publicity and interest, those kids can't be legally qualified as participants."

The official smiled. "I think we'll be safe in giving them a small trophy."

"I'll go along with that," said the director. He stared at the boats disappearing up the river. "Whatever became of that black boat that nearly crashed into some of the boats yesterday? I don't see it registered to participate."

"I was told the San Francisco police reported a bank robbery downtown. It was thought the bandits escaped in a black powerboat."

The director looked confused. "What happened to them?"

"Nobody seems to know," the official said with a shrug. "It's as though they disappeared into thin air."

Lacey studied the charts in her lap, now splattered by all the water that had been thrown into the cockpit of the boat. "A sweeping turn coming up," she alerted

Casey. "Then it's under the Sinclair Freeway bridge and into the mouth of the river."

"It will be nice to enjoy the smoother water ahead," said Casey, happy the river was flatter than the water in San Francisco Bay. He felt as if he and *Hotsy Totsy* were one. The boat and he had created a rhythm. The big Wright aircraft engine was running smoothly without a miss, and as time went on, the speedy little craft increased her pace, working her way through the fleet until she was passing boat after boat.

"How do we stand?" asked Casey.

Lacey made a rough count of the boats she could see up the bay. "Twenty-eighth, we've moved up to twenty-eighth."

Ahead, two more boats were limping off the course. The red boat *Rum Tum Tum* had sucked up a plastic bag from the water into its cooling system, and *Tin Lizzie* was having mechanical problems. So on they went. Now they were twenty-sixth.

Hotsy Totsy pulled even with the blue-and-gold-striped powerboat that had become her nemesis. One minute *Zippity Doo* forged in front, then *Hotsy Totsy*, then *Zippity Doo*. Together, Casey and the magical powerboat made a wide fast turn to line up a heading between two yellow buoys that marked the race course into the bay. *Zippity Doo* stayed right with her.

Casey began to think *Hotsy Totsy* was merely playing with the other boat. The crowds of people lining the shore were madly cheering the varnished mahogany hull to pull ahead of the brilliantly painted powerboat. They were hypnotized by the spectacular action and glamour of speed.

Each boat would take the lead and then lose it. *Zippity Doo*'s pilot pulled every trick in the book to outdistance *Hotsy Totsy* but couldn't gain the lead for more than a mile before Casey forged past.

They were catching up to the main fleet and passing other boats strung out along the course. Their crews were stunned to see an old V-shaped hull battling it out with a modern, carbon-fiber-hulled boat powered by a one-thousand-horsepower, turbocharged engine. *Hotsy Totsy* had pulled ahead of *Zippity Doo*, which was in hot pursuit. To the growing astonishment of *Zippity Doo*'s pilot and copilot, they found themselves losing ground.

"The river is beginning to narrow," Lacey yelled into Casey's ear. "A red buoy is coming up on your port side."

"I see it," Casey yelled back. "We're about to enter the Deep Water Ship Channel, which lets big ships sail up to Sacramento."

"Yes, I see on the map that it's a canal thirty feet deep, two hundred feet wide and forty-three miles long."

"The race goes up the ship channel to the state capital before we return to San Francisco Bay by racing down the river course."

"The channel is clear. They must have stopped all the river traffic."

"Good thing all the tugboats and barges were tied along the shore until the race is over," said Casey. "I'd hate to chase other boats around them."

"The best I can guess is that we're in twenty-first position."

10

The Dash up the Channel to Sacramento

The ship channel banks rose fifteen feet above the water, and the course marker buoys were spaced with barely enough room for three boats to pass through at the same time. The fact that they were being squeezed into a tight group was creating chaos. Boats were knocking against each other. But the worst was yet to come.

The channel closed and tightened to where the banks were only a hundred yards apart.

"What's happening?" said Casey, becoming alarmed. "The river has become no wider than a football field. There's hardly enough room for two boats to pass."

"We're through the entrance to the Sacramento River," explained Lacey, reading her navigation charts. "The race course runs north up the Deep Water Ship Channel, which circles through Sacramento City, and then we race down the actual river back into San Francisco Bay and the finish line."

Casey was frustrated. "Just when *Hotsy Totsy* was running like a winner, we get stuck in a narrow channel that's almost impossible to pass."

But pass *Hotsy Totsy* did. With Casey gaining confidence, she passed five more boats on the long straight up the Deep Water Ship Channel, cutting around hull to hull until Lacey was certain they had scraped the varnish off *Hotsy Totsy*'s beautifully polished mahogany.

By the time they saw the Sacramento skyline and the gold dome above the state capitol, they had crossed the city limit line and *Hotsy Totsy* was in twelfth place.

An official yacht came into view with a large yellow flag on its masthead.

"What's the yellow flag for?" Casey wondered aloud.

"I think they want all the boats to slow down," said Lacey.

In another mile another official yacht was flying a red flag. Small boats were stationed along the course waving the race boats into a small channel where a series of gas trucks were waiting to refuel the race participants at a ship loading dock.

"It's a refueling stop," said Lacey.

"The race officials will catch us for sure now," Casey said grimly. "They won't let us back in the race once we tie up to the dock."

As they slowed down under the caution and red flags, Lacey pointed excitedly at the thousands of people crowding the banks of the river. The word about the children and the old powerboat had swept up and down the river like a tornado. The throng was shouting and cheering madly.

"Look, look!" she said in awe. "They're all cheering for us."

Along the banks of the river, a crowd of children were holding up signs that read:

GO, HOTSY TOTSY!

and another:

YOU CAN WIN, HOTSY TOTSY, YOU CAN WIN!

and another:

DO IT, HOTSY TOTSY!

but the one that almost made Casey and Lacey most happy read:

WE LUV YOU, HOTSY TOTSY AND YOUR DOG TOO!

The twins were stunned at the reception. They had no idea that they had become a national hero and heroine. Many people were even throwing flowers in the water in front of the boat. Television news cameras lined the shores, while helicopters flashed overhead shooting the scene as they trailed the leading boats to the refueling dock.

Downriver, the Boss and his henchmen watched the show, their phantom black boat hidden among a sea of reeds along the shoreline.

"I can't believe those foolish spectators are actually

cheering those bratty little vermin. I can't believe they were allowed to race."

"They look like they're running a good race," said the Beard.

"Yeah," mumbled Wrinkle Face. "I bet they're sorry they can never win."

"Who asked you!" snapped the Boss. "C'mon, get ready. They'll be coming by soon, and then we'll show them what sorry is."

A helicopter settled down onto the end of the dock and the race officials from the marina stepped out. The fat men wearing the white, pink, black and green caps in their blue blazers and carrying clipboards didn't look happy. They huddled in what looked like a serious conversation while staring in the direction of *Hotsy Totsy*.

"We're in a dilemma," said White Cap, the jowls on his face twitching.

"No doubt about it," said Pink Cap, his droopy eyes squinting. "Our backs are to the wall."

"We have to make a decision," said the kindly man under the green cap.

Black Cap took his cap off and wiped a handkerchief over his bald head. "Because of the vast publicity, we have to allow those crazy kids to continue in the race. They've become the darlings of the news media and the American public."

"He's right," said Pink Cap. "If we pulled their boat out of the contest, the crowds would go crazy and might get unruly."

" Then it's settled," said White Cap, who was the head official. "We have to let them continue in the race."

"With luck," said Green Cap, " their old boat will break down and they'll drop out."

"With luck," White Cap echoed. "But we had no

idea they were as fast as they've shown they are and would pass so many of the fastest powerboats ever built."

"Luck," said Black Cap. "They've been lucky. Their luck can't last."

"I agree," said White Cap. "It's a miracle their boat has lasted this far."

"She'll never make it down the river to the bay," agreed Pink Cap. "Few boats will be able to race down a narrow river with sharp bends every mile."

Black Cap nodded. "Twenty failed to make it back to the finish line in last year's race."

"Then it's agreed," said White Cap. "We'll let the *Hotsy Totsy* run the rest of the race. But . . ." He held up his hand. "Since she and the children do not meet race regulations, she cannot be considered for any prize money."

"We all concur," White Cap said, nodding. "*Hotsy*

Totsy is not a true participant but only an intruder who is allowed by our good grace."

All the officials muttered agreement.

A man in white coveralls holding the nozzle of a hose that ran to a fuel tank yelled down to the twins, still in the cockpit beside the dock. "You guys open your fuel cap and I'll fill her up."

Casey looked up. "No, thanks, we don't need any."

The fuel man looked like he hadn't heard right. "How can you not need fuel? You just raced a hundred miles from San Francisco. All the other boats' tanks are nearly empty."

"We're fine and dandy," said Lacey. "Thank you all the same."

"We have enough to get back to San Francisco," Casey assured him.

The fuel man walked over to the next boat, shaking his head.

Lacey whispered to Casey, "No one knows *Hotsy Totsy* is a magical boat and doesn't need fuel for her engine."

"I only hope we can all finish the race in one piece," Casey said quietly. "From what I see on your charts, the river that runs down to the bay is filled with sharp, narrow bends. Passing other boats will be tricky."

Casey and Lacey tensed as the white-capped official and his assistants approached *Hotsy Totsy*. He looked sternly at the twins. "You've run a good race and we've decided to let you continue."

"You mean we can compete and cross the finish line in San Francisco?" asked Lacey doubtfully.

White Cap nodded. "Yes, but since you are not an official entry, you cannot win any trophy or prize money should you finish in the top ten."

"That's fine," said Casey, vastly relieved. "Thank you."

"Just watch your driving, stay out of the way of the

faster boats and don't cause any accidents," the official said severely. "Mind that you stay out of trouble."

"We'll do our best to run a safe race," Casey promised.

The friendly man under the green cap said, "I wish you the best of luck." He turned and gestured at the throng of *Hotsy Totsy* well-wishers crowding the city streets along the river and on the pleasure boats anchored along the race course. "You've certainly become winners in the public's eyes. You and your dog and your boat are featured on every channel on television."

The twins could see a horde of news media television cameras pointed in their direction.

They looked at each other with the same thought. What if their father and mother saw them? If so, they were in for a harsh scolding when they returned to the farm.

11

Danger down the River

From the marina to the delta, the Sacramento River was very curvy and narrow. The race officials wouldn't allow the powerboats to race across the starting line all bunched up. So they started them off one at a time in single file.

Lacey glanced at a list and numbers of the boats in the race before studying her chart of the river. "You'll have to be careful," she said to Casey. "The river width is less than a football field. Until we reach the delta and head into the bay, the water is quite shallow, rarely deeper than nine feet, so you'll have to stay well away from the banks and steer down the middle."

"How far to San Francisco?" Casey asked.

"I'd guess about ninety miles."

Suddenly, Lacey pointed ahead. "We're next," she said, trembling with growing excitement. Because Casey and Lacey and *Hotsy Totsy* crossed the halfway mark in twelfth position, they had to wait behind the eleventh boat in line, a bright white boat with a blue stripe up the middle called *Boom Voom.* The *Boom Voom*'s great rooster tail spray fanned the air and the roar from her engine exhaust crackled. She began tearing down the river chasing the ten boats in front of her.

The crowd along the shore like around the marina were all shouting encouragement to the two children and dog in the beautiful, shiny mahogany powerboat. Everyone waved and held up signs and cheered them on.

"Everybody ready?" said Casey, his knuckles gripped around the steering wheel.

Lacey could only nod, but Floopy barked joyously.

The official swept the green flag in the air with a great flourish. Casey responded by pushing the pedal to the floor. *Hotsy Totsy* shot ahead as if fired from a cannon, her propeller whipping the water into froth that swirled in a spreading fan behind her stern. Her bow raised until it was pointing at the horizon as her keel carved through the Sacramento River, which twisted like a snake toward the sea.

Casey's tight grip on the wheel soon loosened until his fingertips lightly touched the rim as *Hotsy Totsy* dodged the snags that were the contorted remains of tree trunks and branches rising up out of the water, threatening to tear a great gash in her hull if she crashed into one. Through her magical sense, she knew where the shallow water and the underwater snags were hiding and avoided them. Casey simply nodded and now held the wheel gently as *Hotsy Totsy* swung around the other race boats.

Sandbars had to be circled and passed. Many of the sandbars lifted from the riverbed and couldn't be seen under the water surface until it was too late. With her magical sense *Hotsy Totsy* skirted the unseen hazards.

"Keep an eye out for rough spots," shouted Lacey. "You can see where the river current churns around shallow water."

The words no sooner came out of her mouth than *Boom Boom,* now only fifty yards ahead, lurched to a sudden stop as its hull slammed onto a sandbar. As *Hotsy Totsy* soared past, Casey and Lacey saw the pilot and his copilot leap into the barely submerged silt and struggle to push their powerboat into deeper water.

"Now we're eleventh," said Casey as *Hotsy Totsy*

leaned on the side of her hull as she sped around a sharp curve in the river.

"I judge the next boat to be about thirty seconds ahead," Lacey said, shading her eyes with one hand while staring into the afternoon sun toward the west.

Casey's fingers lightly tapped the rim of the steering wheel as *Hotsy Totsy* ducked around a tree stump that was floating in the river current. "We'll catch it," he replied, "right after the next bend."

The Sacramento River curled east of town. Thousands of people sat comfortably on blankets and in lawn chairs, having a picnic as they watched the race. As one they all stood when they spotted *Hotsy Totsy* speeding past and flung their arms in the air as if urging her on.

Roads ran along both banks of the river. Many cars had stopped to watch the boats speed by. The buildings and houses of the city soon dropped behind and the crowds thinned. The land beyond the river-banks became fields planted with what Casey and Lacey, being farm kids, quickly recognized as chilies, beans and cabbage. While Casey focused his attention on speeding around the bends of the river, Lacey looked up and marveled at flights of white pelicans gliding just inches above the water, ignoring the boats zooming past and the thunderous roar of their exhaust.

Floopy yapped at a blue heron that stood on spindly legs, his claws clutched around a branch of a walnut tree that hung over the river. He seemed fascinated by the blur of colors that flashed past.

"Here they come," the Boss declared, peering from his black phantom boat, which was hidden in the reeds.

"They're going awful fast," said the Beard.

"Real fast," added Wrinkle Face.

"Our boat is faster than any in the race," said the Boss with a smug grin.

"The Boss will fix 'em," said Wrinkle Face.

"Yeah, he'll fix 'em," came back the Beard.

"They'll never know what hit them," the Boss muttered in growing fury.

He waited until the twins passed before he jammed his foot down on the pedal, sending the black boat rocketing into the center of the river behind *Hotsy Totsy*'s wake.

Hotsy Totsy was closing on a boat painted white with a lightning-shaped red stripe along its hull. Lacey checked the list of boats and saw that its name was *Toot Toot Tootsie*. She had slender and graceful lines and was setting a fast pace, rapidly coming up on the boats in front of her. Her pilot turned and saw *Hotsy Totsy* charging up like a racehorse around the far turn.

Casey backed off the throttle pedal to keep *Hotsy Totsy*'s bow from striking *Toot Toot Tootsie*'s stern. The sudden move saved the twins, their dog and the magical boat from an unforeseen disaster.

In the blink of an eye the phantom black boat shot past in front of them. The Boss misjudged the distance between the two boats just as Casey took his foot off the throttle pedal. Instead, the Boss rammed his boat into the stern of *Toot Toot Tootsie*, cutting the boat in two just ahead of the engine. *Toot Toot Tootsie*'s bow soared out of the water as the engine with its prop still wildly spinning sank into the depths of the river.

Luckily, the pilot and his copilot were thrown clear and swiftly swam toward the riverbank, where people were wading out into the water to help them ashore.

"Curses!" grumbled the Boss. "I'll get those brats yet." He spun the wheel and cut in front of *Hotsy Totsy* in another attempt to smash into her.

"Oh no!" Lacey moaned. "It's the Boss and his henchmen."

"Where did they come from?" Casey wondered aloud.

"They must have been hiding off the river waiting to crush us and destroy *Hotsy Totsy*."

Casey could see that the Beard said something to the Boss, who then began whipping his boat from side to side in an attempt to block the twins and *Hotsy Totsy* from passing and getting away.

Casey tried to back off the throttle and stay behind the black phantom, but *Hotsy Totsy* was determined to pass and locked the throttle pedal. She steered to their right to confuse the Boss but suddenly swung around to the left and bounced high in the air as she climbed over the wave caused by the black phantom's wake. *Hotsy Totsy* smacked down again with a huge splash as she pulled alongside just as both boats entered a tight, narrow bend in the river.

Hotsy Totsy was fighting the black phantom hard. Neither boat gave an inch. Together, Casey and Lacey held their breath. They twisted around the bend hull to hull. Casey was sure he could have reached out and touched the Boss, who was trying to shove them against a dead tree standing out from the shoreline fifty yards ahead. Then, reaching deep within her magical powers, *Hotsy Totsy* twisted and cut around the turn, tearing through the water while leaning on the side of her hull.

If not for their safety belts and harnesses, Casey and Lacey would surely have been thrown out of the boat. But just as they thought *Hotsy Totsy* was going to flip upside down, she flattened out and surged ahead, leaving the phantom black boat bouncing in her wake.

Lacey felt numb for a few moments until she regained her poise and confidence. She turned around and saw the Boss shaking his fist at them as he slowly began to fall behind.

"From now on," she lectured Casey, "you pass on a straight stretch of river. No more overtaking on bends."

"*Hotsy Totsy* is in control," Casey said as they rounded the next bend and set off after two boats about a quarter of a mile in front of their bow. "She won't let us down. The Boss will never catch us now. We're faster."

A short distance ahead a yellow boat and a gray boat were racing side by side, neither giving the other the slightest advantage. As they came closer, Casey could see that their pilots, like others before, were not about to let *Hotsy Totsy* pass. They were approaching a dock that extended nearly a hundred feet in the river. Small boats were moored along the sides while a crowd of spectators stood on the wooden planks.

Suddenly and without warning, the yellow boat struck a snag that was lurking just beneath the water. The tree's trunk ripped a long hole in the bottom of the boat's hull, and it began to quickly sink as if it was a diving submarine. The pilot and the copilot jumped into the river just before the boat disappeared under the water. They looked unhurt and floated comfortably in their life jackets while waiting to be rescued.

Casey was going to stop and pick up the floating boat racers, but Lacey shouted, "Never mind them! Head for the dock! Hurry!"

Her voice had such a sound of urgency that Casey didn't ask why. He spun the wheel, but *Hotsy Totsy* sensed something was wrong and had already turned sharply and sped toward the dock. Out of the corner of his eye he saw the Boss and his black phantom boat zoom past.

Seconds later, Lacey waved her hands and cried, "Stop here!"

The magical speedboat came to an immediate stop. Then before Casey and Floopy knew what was happening, Lacey unclasped her safety harness and leaped over the side of the boat. She dove under the surface of the water beside the dock and disappeared.

The people on the dock were stunned. They couldn't understand why a boat speeding downriver would all of a sudden race up to the dock while ignoring the men floating in the river.

Lacey was a good swimmer and could hold her breath for a long time. Over a minute passed as excitement grew on the dock when she didn't immediately appear. Then a woman began screaming and pointing into the water.

At first no one knew why she was screaming and acting so crazy. Then Lacey's head appeared, and she lifted her arms out of the water. She was holding a little boy in her hands. Every race spectator had been watching the powerboat sink, and none had noticed

DANGER DOWN THE RIVER

the little boy fall off the dock, even his own mother. No one, that is, except Lacey, who just so happened to be looking at the dock when the boy splashed into the river.

The dock was too high for her to hand him to the people above, so she gave him to Casey, who lifted him into *Hotsy Totsy* and held him upside down as he coughed out the water he had swallowed. When the boy began crying, everyone knew he was all right and sighed happily. Casey stood on the seat of the speedboat and raised the little boy up to his grateful mother on the dock.

"Oh, thank you," she said, tears flowing from her eyes. "Thank you for saving my little boy."

"My sister, Lacey, gets the credit," said Casey honestly as he helped a thoroughly drenched Lacey back into the boat.

"I'm only happy I was lucky enough to see him fall into the river," Lacey told the mother.

"Nice going, sis," Casey said, smiling. "I'm proud of you."

Lacey smiled back and made an attempt to arrange her water-soaked hair.

"You were the only one," Casey said, his voice turning serious. "If it wasn't for you, the little boy would have surely drowned."

Lacey pointed over the windshield. "Look," she said as an official race boat moved toward the men in the water.

One of the yachts used to monitor the race was slowing down to rescue the floating powerboat team in the water. None of the other powerboats or their pilots had stopped to help. They roared around the men in the water as though they didn't exist.

"We've fallen back in the pack," said Casey. "At least six boats have passed us since we stopped."

"The Boss went by too," Lacey said.

Casey nodded. "He didn't dare attack us in front

of so many people. He's down the river, waiting to pounce on us again."

"This time we'll be on our guard."

Wasting no more words, Casey turned *Hotsy Totsy* back toward the center of the river and pushed hard on the throttle pedal. The big Wright aircraft engine howled as it went to full power. The prop dug into the water, lifting the bow, and *Hotsy Totsy* rocketed back into the race.

12

The Dash to the Finish Line

Floopy stood with his rear paws on the seat and his front paws on the instrument cowling, his tail wagging wildly as if it was conducting a band. Lacey studied her chart of the river and warned Casey when a sharp bend in the river was coming close. Casey and Floopy kept their eyes ahead, looking for any sign of the black phantom boat hiding in the bushes along the shore.

Although Casey had his hands on the steering helm, it seemed to move without him turning the rudder. *Hotsy Totsy* was flying down the river, passing one, sometimes two boats on the straight stretches, then curving into a bend at full speed until the edge of the cockpit was only inches above the water. Casey gripped the wheel, but Lacey and Floopy had to hold on for dear life, hoping their seat belts were secure.

Sometimes *Hotsy Totsy*, ignoring Lacey's pleas, cut around a boat while going through a bend. Swerving with her keel almost out of the water, throwing up a high rooster tail of water behind her stern, she skidded around her competitors as if she was attached to underwater railroad tracks.

The people onshore stood in awe as *Hotsy Totsy* with the two children and a funny-looking dog with a leather helmet and goggles came and went, the roar of the big V-12 Wright engine booming out of the twin exhaust pipes in the stern like thunder. Vroom, vroom, vroom! The faces on the other race pilots reflected shock, disbelief and finally amazement at the daring antics of the antique boat as it darted past them.

As they hurtled through another turn, Lacey yelled,

"After we pass the bend at the end of the next straight, we'll enter the upper bay."

"Still no sign of the Boss?" Casey shouted back.

"No, but I'm sure we haven't seen the last of him," Lacey said, staring downriver.

The words had no sooner been spoken than the black phantom boat, with the Boss at the helm, shot from behind a big rock and came roaring up the river on a collision course with *Hotsy Totsy*. The twins had no doubt the Boss would be merciless.

Closer and closer the two boats shot toward the other. Neither slowing. The Boss was pushing the black phantom as fast as it would go. Casey didn't have to hold the pedal down. *Hotsy Totsy*'s great Wright engine was running as fast as it would go. For a few seconds time seemed to slow, and Casey and Lacey thought this might be the end. Floopy stared at the black phantom boat and snarled.

A hundred yards, then fifty. The twins could clearly see the faces of the Boss and his henchmen. Twenty-five yards came and went, and the speeding boats were only fifty feet apart when *Hotsy Totsy* lifted her bow and soared out of the river and flew over the black phantom boat. The Boss and his henchmen looked skyward, eyes wide, mouths hanging open as the spinning prop whirred by overhead. They watched dumbly as the antique boat bounced back into the water with a massive splash beyond the Boss's boat.

Casey was afraid the propeller might fly off when it came out of the water as the engine raced uncontrollably, but it held on to the driveshaft without letting go. Within minutes, the black phantom boat was nearly a quarter of a mile behind *Hotsy Totsy*.

"Blast those brats and their crazy boat," the enraged Boss roared, shaking his fist at *Hotsy Totsy* as she sped down the river toward the bay.

"We'd better forget them kids," cautioned Wrinkle Face, "and make our getaway."

"Yeah," said the Beard. "The cops will be waiting and watching for our black boat when we come into the bay."

"No!" the Boss roared. "That old boat will never last on the rough waters of the bay. It's probably already coming apart. We'll finish the brats off before they cross the finish line."

Casey and Lacey passed under a high bridge and darted into the upper part of San Francisco Bay. The wind had come up and blew in through the Golden Gate from the sea. The water became choppy and the keel began to bounce over the incoming waves.

"How many boats can you see ahead of us?" asked Casey, wiping the spray from his eyes.

Lacey squinted across the water toward the Richmond–San Rafael Bridge. "I see four. Two battling for first place and two trailing in their wakes no more than a hundred yards ahead."

"I can't believe we caught them so fast." He patted the instrument panel. "Good old *Hotsy Totsy*, she just won't give up."

Although she had set a marvelous pace, the pressure was still on. Once they passed under the Richmond–San Rafael Bridge, the finish line was less than ten miles away. Casey kept the foot pedal pressed to the floor. Just as they pulled up alongside a sleek green and gold boat called the *Jingle Jangle*, they both hit an incoming wave and were launched into the air. It was a heart-stopping few moments as *Hotsy Totsy* and *Jingle Jangle* flew nearly a hundred feet until their keels smacked the water hard.

The *Jingle Jangle* wasn't so lucky as one of her propeller blades broke off and the driver cut the throttle so that the boat still had forward motion but was only moving at twenty miles an hour.

The driver and his co-driver waved graciously with encouragement as the twins sped past.

The next boat in front of them was the apricot orange *Rat Tat Tat*. Soon they were leaping over the waves that spread behind the other boat and closing on its stern.

"Don't get too close," Lacey warned her brother.

"Never fear," answered Casey with a grin. "That's the driver who splashed us by coming too close. Now it's our turn. I'm going to show him what *Hotsy Totsy* can really do."

At what seemed the last second, Casey swung the wheel and whipped the boat around until he was almost on top of *Rat Tat Tat*'s stern. Then he cut a slight turn and leaped ahead until only a few inches separated the hulls of the two speeding boats. In shocked surprise, the other driver turned and stared wide-eyed at Casey, not believing the old mahogany boat could have matched his speed.

Casey smiled and gave a short wave like a salute and shouted, "We'll wait for you at the finish."

As soon as he said the words, *Hotsy Totsy* leaped ahead, her bow two feet out of the water as her propeller thrust her ahead. The wash from her wake soaked the crew and drenched *Rat Tat Tat* in a huge sheet of water. Lacey laughed and waved at the driver and his engineer, who had no choice but to endure the tidal wave as *Hotsy Totsy* pulled ahead and soon left them a hundred yards behind.

Lacey pointed over the windshield as Alcatraz Island came into view. "Only two boats are ahead of us," she said in Casey's ear.

"We're gaining on them," Casey yelled back, his excitement growing.

"Yes, we are, but it's only four miles to the finish line."

"*Hotsy Totsy* will catch them," Casey said, his heart

leaping with confidence, sure that his magical boat was up to the task.

They shot across the bay and within the next mile were only twenty yards behind the sterns of the blue-and-gold-striped *Zippity Doo* and the red *Dragon Fire.* Casey knew he could catch and pass them before the finish line. But the twins were desperately tired now after the long, hard hours of the race. The waves sweeping across San Francisco Bay were hard on the boat and their bodies. Lacey felt water over her ankles on the bottom of the cockpit. She realized the seams of the mahogany planking had taken a terrible beating and were coming loose, allowing water to seep in and slosh around the lower hull.

"We're taking on water!" Lacey shouted over the thunder of the three boats and their engines.

Casey felt the water over his shoes too and looked down. Now he could see it flowing between the loosened planks of the hull. His first thought was to slow down and save the boat.

But then he looked back across the bay and saw that the finish line was only a mile away.

"Stop, stop!" Lacey pleaded. "*Hotsy Totsy* can't take any more. She'll surely sink before we reach shore if we don't slow down."

Casey knew she was right. "We can't risk losing *Hotsy Totsy*."

Just as he lifted his foot from the throttle pedal a large wave curled in through the Golden Gate and swept across the bay. The two boats ahead were thrown sideways, having caught the wave broadside. Up, up they went, tossed into the air like two toothpicks. *Zippity Doo* spun around and fell across the bow of the *Dragon Fire* in what is called a T-bone as they crashed back into the water. *Dragon Fire* was driven under the surface like a submarine as water gushed through her smashed bow and into her engine compartment. The shock was so heavy both men on her crew had their helmets torn away.

The bottom hull of *Zippity Doo* looked as if it exploded; debris flew everywhere. Her great engine was torn from its mounts and dropped through the huge gash in the hull to the bottom of the bay, still running at full revolutions as it disappeared beneath the waves.

Hotsy Totsy went over hard when the wave crashed against her starboard bow. To Lacey it all seemed to happen in slow motion, the crash of the two boats ahead, the smash of the wave against the boat. She felt the boat twist onto its side, and she thought they were going over. She clutched Floopy, who growled at the wave as though it was alive.

Casey held on to the wheel and worked hard to turn it. Amazingly, *Hotsy Totsy* responded, and her bow swung over the wave crest. The little speedboat was hurled into the air and fell back with a hard impact as it came to a stop in the water, which was now littered with the scattered remains of what had been two beautiful powerboats. All the crew members had been thrown from their cockpits into the water. Only one could barely raise his hand to let them know he was alive. The other three men floated in their survival gear and appeared to be unconscious.

"We've got to help them," cried Lacey.

Casey looked across the water and saw rescue boats speeding toward the crash scene. But they were more than two miles away. "Let's help the ones who look unconscious," he replied in an even tone, "before they drown."

"We're too little to drag them on board," said Lacey.

Casey shook his head. "No, we'll help keep them afloat with their heads out of the water till help arrives. We might cause them more injury if we tried to drag them into the cockpit."

Without another word, Casey steered *Hotsy Totsy* toward the two crew members from the *Dragon Fire*, who were floating motionless. Casey stopped the boat alongside, leaned over the side of the boat and helped Lacey hold the men's heads above water. Floopy even helped by clamping his teeth on one of the men's life jackets and pulling so that the man's head was clear and he could breathe without swallowing water.

Casey eased the boat toward the man who weakly waved. "Can you hold on?" he said.

"I can make it," the *Zippity Doo*'s driver said faintly. "Save my friend."

"Not to worry," Casey assured him.

The other man was floating only ten yards away. Casey moved *Hotsy Totsy* alongside and eased the man's head slightly back so that his mouth and nose were out of the water.

"How are they?" Casey asked Lacey.

"Injured but breathing," she answered. "How about yours?"

"A hard knock on the head, but he should be all right in a few days."

They heard the roar from the engine of an approaching boat. Casey glanced up to see what powerboat was about to roar past. His heart skipped a beat when he recognized the black phantom boat with the Boss hunched over the steering wheel, steering in a straight line toward *Hotsy Totsy.*

"The Boss!" he shouted to Lacey. "He's going to ram us."

"He can't!" Lacey cried. "We're holding on to injured men."

They both knew the Boss could have cared less. He intended to shatter *Hotsy Totsy* and send her and the twins and their dog to the bottom of San Francisco Bay.

The Boss and his black phantom boat and evil

henchmen were coming fast when suddenly a large boat came at an angle, then struck them a glancing blow and shoved them aside into clear water before they could crash into *Hotsy Totsy* and the injured crews.

"Put up your hands!" shouted a voice through a bullhorn from what turned out to be a big police boat. "You're under arrest!"

Seeing there was no hope of escaping a heavily armed police boat, the Boss shut down his engine and let the phantom boat drift.

"Curses!" he snarled, striking the cowling with his fist. "Foiled again."

"Oh no," moaned the Beard. "It's back to prison."

"I don't want to go back," wailed Wrinkle Face.

"The warden from the prison in Nevada where you escaped will be glad to see you robbers behind bars once again," said the policeman on the boat.

"At least it won't be Alcatraz," said the Boss, looking back at the cold, dark rock.

"Throw over that suitcase with the bank's money," ordered the policeman. "Then come on board with your hands outstretched for the handcuffs."

"Next time it will be a different story," the Boss said wickedly, his eyes filled with menace. "Those brats will pay for standing in the way of the Boss."

Within minutes, the rescue boats had arrived, and the paramedics jumped into the water and helped move the injured powerboat crew onto stretchers before gently lifting them aboard. "Nice work, kids," one of the rescuers said. "Are any of you hurt?"

"A few bumps and bruises, but we're okay," replied Lacey.

"Can we take you on board? It looks like your boat is taking on water."

Casey stared down at the water sloshing around in the bottom of the boat. "She'll get us to shore," he answered.

"Good luck to you," the rescuer shouted, waving

as his boat began speeding toward the nearest dock and a waiting ambulance.

"Are we sinking?" asked Lacey.

Casey simply nodded as he leaned over the side and gazed forward. A jagged piece of blue metal was penetrating the bow below the waterline. "It looks like we struck a piece of *Zippity Doo* when she blew apart."

"So that's where the water is coming from," said Lacey, her voice touched with fear. "We must get to shore quickly."

Casey sat behind the steering wheel for a moment, his face set in grim determination. "Not before we cross the finish line," he said steadfastly. "*Hotsy Totsy* is going to finish the race."

He pressed the throttle and the speedboat began roaring across the water again.

"We'll sink before we reach shore," Lacey protested.

"Not if our speed lifts the bow high enough so it's out of the water."

Almost when he spoke, *Hotsy Totsy*'s small, arrow-like bow rose slowly above the water as she bravely rushed forward in what looked like a futile attempt to keep from sinking.

Hotsy Totsy was more than a wooden watercraft with a big powerful engine. She had a heart. She vibrated with a driving spirit that would never give up. It was as though she had a life of her own. Spray from her wake flew like a cloudburst of rain. Her exhaust rumbled like thunder. She began traveling across the waves faster than she had ever soared before, plowing over the small waves while meeting the large ones head-on and crashing through their crests.

The drivers of the other boats speeding toward the finish line couldn't believe such an old boat could dart across the water in a blur of spray. Spectators lining the shore and the docks and even those on boats in the water began yelling and waving them on. Fireboats were shooting water high into the air as the police rescue boats rushed alongside, their sirens blending with horns and whistles sounding across the bay. Thousands of people who had come to love the twins, their dog and their wondrous boat were cheering them wildly.

Casey and Lacey and their beloved boat couldn't win the race, but they could finish in grand style.

As they dashed across the finish line, a race official stood on the cabin roof of a huge yacht and excitedly waved the checkered flag. It was when Casey didn't slow down but kept *Hotsy Totsy* running at full speed that everyone realized the boat was sinking. The bow was lower in the water, and the hull was settling toward the deck cowling. A moan went up from the crowd, followed by a hushed silence as the boat raced toward a narrow beach between the marina docks.

They could see now that Lacey was madly bailing

water over the side with Casey's baseball cap as fast as she could splash it into the air. The boat looked as if it was going to slide beneath the water at any minute.

The water inside the boat had risen over the twins' feet and inches away from their knees. Floopy's basset hound eyes took on a woeful look as he stood with his paws against the instrument panel so he wouldn't have to sit in the water that was coming over the seat.

"We won't make it," Lacey said gravely.

Casey stared at the beach, now no more than a hundred yards away. "*Hotsy Totsy* won't let us down," he said bravely. "She'll get us there."

He could see it was going to be a very near thing. The bow had fallen until it was parting the water like a cleaver and the speed had dropped off alarmingly. A boat nearly filled with water couldn't go fast despite its powerful engine, which began to cough and sputter as the water sloshed around the electrical system.

A fleet of spectator boats had crowded around the sinking *Hotsy Totsy*, shouting encouragement and urging Casey and Lacey to save themselves and abandon the boat. They couldn't believe the magical speedboat was thrusting forward against such unbelievable odds. Hope was in their hearts, but fear was in their minds.

Hotsy Totsy was driving hard, but the weight of the water pulling her under the surface cut her speed down to only ten miles an hour. The shore seemed close enough to touch, but the twins knew it was out of reach. Just when all seemed lost, there came a bump and the boat shuddered. Then it came to an abrupt stop that threw Floopy over the windshield into the water.

"A sandbar off the beach!" shouted Casey excitedly. "We've run onto a sandbar off the beach."

Hotsy Totsy responded with a tremendous surge that pushed her up and onto the sandbar until she was high and dry above the water and the danger of sinking under the depths had faded away.

"She did it!" Lacey cried happily, hugging Casey around the neck. "She saved herself."

"How did we do? Were you able to see how many boats passed us?"

"Five," said Lacey. "Only five beat us across the finish line. If we hadn't stopped to rescue those men after the accident, we might have won."

Casey raised his hands and shrugged. "No regrets," he said with a slight smile. "We did what we had to do. Some things are more important than winning a race." He turned off the engine and was surprised at the roar that remained in his ears.

The twins had forgotten about Floopy until he began barking. Boats were drifting around *Hotsy Totsy*, staying safely away from the sandbar, their passengers cheering madly at seeing the old wooden boat and her crew safe and sound. Many people who were on the beach swam out from shore. One teenage boy helped lift Floopy onto the boat. Floopy, who was happy to be back on board, stood on the cowling in front of the windshield and shook the water from his fur in a great curtain of spray.

A small boat motored over from the big official yacht and picked up the twins and Floopy.

It was a beautiful old mahogany boat about the same age as *Hotsy Totsy*. It carried them over to the yacht, where they were helped on board.

Boatloads of reports and photographers surrounded the yacht while helicopters with TV camera crews hovered overhead. Spectators on a fleet of small boats, yachts and passenger boats swarmed around the official race yacht. Horns tooted, whistles shrieked and people cheered. It was a merry and joyous demonstration.

All the officials greeted them. The kindly man in the green cap shook their hands and Floopy's paw. The chief race official in the white cap smiled as he patted Casey and Lacey on the head. He merely nodded at Floopy.

"Well, well," he said nicely. "You and your boat are the heroes of the hour."

"Our boat deserves most of the credit," said Lacey.

"You saved the little boy who fell off the dock and stopped and rescued three crew members from drowning when you might have ignored them, continued on and won the race."

"Our parents taught us to help other people and do the right thing," said Lacey.

"They taught you well," said the official in the green cap.

"Our boat is in pretty bad shape," Casey said, staring at *Hotsy Totsy*, sitting on the sandbar and surrounded by people who had swum out from shore and boats from the news media, whose crews were shooting photos and taping with TV cameras. "I'd like to see if we can repair it and return home to Castroville."

"Don't worry your little head about your boat," said the chief official. "The race officials arranged for a barge to lift it from the sandbar and have it repaired by people who are experts at restoring old mahogany boats."

"And there's more," said Green Cap. "There's a reward of ten thousand dollars for helping catch the Boss and his henchmen. And on top of that, the bank is offering you another reward of fifteen thousand dollars for helping return their money that was stolen by the Boss."

"Twenty-five thousand dollars," Lacey said with growing excitement. "Our mom and dad can use it to buy new equipment to run the farm."

"And speaking of your mother and father."

He stepped aside, revealing Ima and Ever Nice-folk.

Fear ran through Casey and Lacey, but it quickly melted as the Nicefolks swept their twins up in their arms and kissed them. The scene of warmth and happiness was a sight to see.

Mother and father were happy to see their children happy and unhurt. They were also proud of their amazing accomplishments.

Even Floopy was caught up in the good cheer. He hopped up and down with his tongue hanging out and his tail swirling like a windmill.

Mr. Nicefolk then looked serious and said, "We have to talk when we get home."

"Yes," said Mrs. Nicefolk. "You must never do something like this without our permission."

Then they both laughed and wrapped their arms around the twins and squeezed them tightly.

*   *   *

That night in the Fairmont Hotel on Nob Hill there was a big celebration by all the powerboat crews and the people who supervised the race. During a lavish dinner, the winner's trophy and a check for a hundred thousand dollars were awarded to the crew of the red, white and blue *Uncle Sam*, who had crossed the finish line first.

Then the chief official got up and made a speech, telling how the twins, their dog and their boat, *Hotsy Totsy*, had saved the lives of other crew members as well as the little boy. He also told of their harrowing adventure of being kidnapped by the Boss and escaping his clutches.

When he finished talking, the president of the bank presented Lacey with the fifteen-thousand-dollar check for the return of the bank's stolen money. Then the San Francisco police chief rose and handed Casey the ten-thousand-dollar check for helping apprehend the criminals.

The Nicefolk family embraced, and the audience stood and applauded. Floopy, who sat in a chair at the table in front of a juicy steak with a bone, ignored the festivities and chewed and chewed.

Two days later, *Hotsy Totsy* was restored to her natural beauty. Ima and Ever Nicefold left for the drive home as Casey and Lacey boarded their beloved boat for the voyage to Castroville.

The docks were loaded with well-wishers. The drivers chipped in and bought them a beautiful brass trophy made from a powerboat's big propeller. The engraving on one of the prop blades read:

TO CASEY AND LACEY NICEFOLK
FOR THEIR BRAVERY AND KINDNESS.
IN DEEP APPRECIATION FROM

THE CREWS IN THE GOLD CUP GRAND
NATIONAL POWERBOAT RACE.

Lacey had tears in her eyes while Casey puffed out
his chest as they were handed the trophy.

"Oh, thank you, thank you," Lacey cried as she
kissed the three crew members she and Casey had
saved, who presented them with the trophy.

Finally, after saying their good-byes to the crews
and race officials and accepting the cheers of the
spectators, who had come to love them, their boat
and their dog, the lines were thrown and *Hotsy Totsy*
slowly slipped from the dock and headed toward the
Golden Gate Bridge as a band played "Auld Lang
Syne."

As soon as they motored up the Salinas River to their
farm, Casey shoved the boat onto the magical pad. He
pushed the right lever on the mystery box that made

things smaller. After the purple mist had faded, *Hotsy Totsy* had became a toy model boat again.

"I'm going to miss her," Lacey said sorrowfully.

Casey put his arm around his sister. "We'll make her big again, just as we will *Vin Fiz.*"

Lacey said, "We'll have to tell Mom and Dad our secret."

"We can only hope Mr. Sucoh Sucop won't mind if they know too."

"He won't," said Lacey, her eyes dreamy. "I'm sure of it."

"Then we can make another toy grow big and go off on an adventure."

"Yes," she said, giving her brother a big hug. "There's always another adventure waiting over the horizon."